NOT

FORGOTTEN

New Lenox
Public Library District
120 Veterans Parkway
New Lenox, Illinois 60451

By: Donna M. Zadunajsky

ISBN # 978-1-938037-17-7

3 1984 00314 7954

This novel is a work of fiction. Names, characters,
places and incidents are either the product of the
author's imagination or are used fictitiously. Any
resemblance to actual persons, living or dead, events,
or locales is entirely coincidental.

1

Table of Contents

Novels by Donna M. Zadunajsky

Broken Promises

Children Books written by Donna M.
Zadunajsky
Illustrated by Judith Bicking

Tayla's Best Day Ever!

Tayla's Best Friend

Tayla's New Friend

Tayla goes to Grammie's House

Tayla takes a Trip

Tayla's Day at the Beach

Tayla's First Day of School

Acknowledgments

I would like to express my many thanks and appreciation to Stephanie Barker who helped in some of the research and structuring of this book. And to my dear friend Angie Theodore for reading my second draft and for her insights on what needed fixed. I want to say Thank you to Phyllis Cox, a Proofreader from Writers Digest and to Carolyn Walker, a 2nd Draft Critique editor and last but not least, Kathleen Marusak for going through my final stage of editing. Also to my husband and daughter for pushing me to accomplish my long time dream. Thank you all so much for your help at getting my novel into print.

Part One

Life is full of surprises and serendipity. Being open to unexpected turns in the road is an important part of success. If you try to plan every step, you may miss those wonderful twists and turns. Just find your next adventure-do it well, enjoy it-and then, not now, think about what comes next....   Condoleeza Rice

To fear love is to fear life, and those who fear life are already dead....
Bertrand Russell

1

We all have incidents in our lives that change us, some for the good and others for the bad. Then there are those events that make us into the people we were meant to become. These changes may take weeks, months, or even years, but when they do come, they either come at us head-on or tackle us from behind. What changed my life had tackled me as though I were a quarterback and life, the defense lineman, was just itching to toss me on my ass.

Because of this and what happened when I was young, we had to move from the house I had grown to love. I was turning six years old the day we moved into this house, the place where I now stood. I had pestered my mom into painting the ceiling the color of the sky with stars that sparkled when the lights were off. Granted, my mother was no Leonardo da Vinci, but the woman had the skills to create a resemblance of the magnificence of the evening sky.

I would lie in bed at night and stare at the stars as though they were my dreams waiting to come to life if only I could grab one. These lights of the heavens helped me sleep.

I took to my room after the incident....

My sister Shelia's bedroom was down the hall from mine; she's older than me by two years. She was the kind of sister who would never let me forget who was the oldest. Who, she thought, was superior. We didn't get along until we became adults, though to this day we still have our differences. For some reason that fell through the cracks of my perception, she hated me. Well, I'd have to admit that was the feeling I always got from her. Those times when we were near one another, the sense of friction between us was so strong that sometimes I thought if we moved the wrong way, the sparks would ignite a flame. Hate can be like that; the longer it's held onto, the more flammable it becomes.

She always seemed so much smarter than me and I could tell that she was my parents' favorite; at least that was my impression. No matter what I did, I was never good enough for them. I guess it's something siblings go through when they live under the same roof.

I was fourteen when we moved to a new house in a different town far away from everything we knew, everything that felt right. I was fourteen the day my sister stopped talking to me, her verbal communication becoming that of a caveman with grunts and groans over anything and everything I said. She said it was my fault that we had to leave our friends behind. I should have been more careful that night and trusted my gut feeling. But I was young, and when we are young, we do things because we want to be loved and have people like us. What happened shouldn't have happened to me. Not to anyone.

I turned towards the road as a car passed, its muffler spitting out gray smoke filling the pre-summer air. My eyes caught a glimpse of the FOR SALE sign hammered into the front lawn. Across the front was a sticker reading "SOLD." I strolled up the stone walk and made my way to the front door. The people who owned the house after us had planted lilac bushes along the front. They gave off a sweet smell, and the aroma was enticing. If this house could talk, it would tell you about all the memories shared here, good and bad. It had been almost twenty-six years since I had seen my old home. The people that lived here after us had painted the house an olive green, a huge difference from our choice of buckskin brown. I knew one day I would come back to our old house, but didn't think I would buy it.

Jingling the keys in my hand, I unlocked the door and entered.

Everything looked just as I had imagined it.

The people who bought our house have moved into the city. They hadn't known the amount of time and energy I put into checking the Internet for years, waiting for them to sell. Now I stood in the foyer and soaked in all the old memories.

Feeling uneasy, I was hesitant walking into the living room. The floodgates had opened and memories flowed in and out of my mind. I could remember the dark brown sofa and loveseat we had. Those pieces of furniture felt like my old pair of corduroy jeans and reminded me how those jeans were always soft to the touch and comfortable against the flesh of my legs.

10

The walls were light pineapple yellow, the same color we left them. We would sit for hours in this room, playing games and watching television. The light blue shag carpet we'd had was replaced by a beige Berber carpet with lighter shades of background colors that were pleasing to the eye.

The kitchen sat in the far rear of the house, with the garage off to its side. I can picture my mother cooking us meals and baking cookies and pies. She was a woman of multiple household talents. As a child, I spent many hours working on my homework at the dining room table and helping my mom cook. I wasn't as close to my father as I was to my mother. I just had an inexplicable connection to her. No matter what was on my mind, she would sit down and listen to me. She never interrupted me or even tried to force her opinions on me. We were closer than my sister and I.

Turning, I started up the wooden oak stairs to my old room. It was the last door at the end of the hallway. The door was closed; when I turned the knob, the hinges squeaked as the door swayed open. I flicked on the light to my left and glanced around, my mind flashing back to a time when I was sitting on my bed reading my favorite novel, *Misery*, by Stephen King. My hair was long, thick and black, and I always wore it tied back in a braid that my mother wove for me every morning.

My heart started to race as though I had run up the stairs with more gusto than my body could muster; the memories kept knocking me back into the past while I fought to stay in the present. All those memories of a day when I was lying on my bed and crying now seemed to come to a screeching halt. I didn't tell my parents about that day, at least not right away. I guess I would have to say I was ashamed of what happened that night. I thought maybe I could've prevented it. When we are kids we always think we are right, and our parents are wrong. And whatever they preach, we seem to do the total opposite. I guess that's why they say gaining wisdom is a learning experience. You must fall and make mistakes in order to get back up and try again. I wished with every part of me that I could have told my parents that I now understand what they were trying to do and why they said and did what they did. Being a parent, that's what we do; we give our children unconditional love.

I heard a car door shut outside. Glancing out the window, I turned and jogged down the stairs, and wiped the wetness from my face before opening the door.

"Hey, Sis," I said. "Glad you could come see me."

"Deanna, I wouldn't miss this day in a million years," Shelia replied. "So, are the papers signed? Is this place all yours?"

"Yes, I finished signing them this morning." A smile formed on my lips. We hugged and I moved aside for her to enter. It had been months since I had seen her last. Her hair was blonde and cut just above the ears, and she looked much thinner than she had the last time I saw her. We both now lived in different towns, not close, maybe two hours away. For some reason we never made time to get together, to bond like sisters should. Maybe now that I'd bought this house, we could start over and be the sister to each other that we should've been many years ago.

"Wow, it's been a long time since I've been here," Shelia said.

"Me, too," I replied. "But it's a good feeling to

13

be back in our house again."

"Where's Brent?" she asked.

"Still at school. He has finals this week, and then he'll graduate from eighth grade. He's excited about the move and going to high school out here."

"He'll love our school." Her smile faded, becoming a frown.

I know she still blames me for our moving, but hope one day she will forgive me.

I nodded. "It was a good school. The movers will be here on Friday. Will you be around to help us unpack?"

"You know I will." Shelia turned and tramped up the stairs. I thought to myself that my parents would be proud that I had moved back here to our old house and that Shelia and I were spending more time together.

I've thought about them often since their sudden death. It was a brisk fall morning; I was out on my morning jog when fire trucks raced by me with their sirens blaring. When I saw the red truck turn down the street my parents lived on, I decided to follow them. As I rounded the corner, I could feel the heat against my skin, the flames burning hot and fast.

It was then that I realized my parents' house was on fire. When I ran up to the house a police officer grabbed me and held me back. I was kicking and screaming as he held me tighter. I pleaded with him to save them, but he said there was nothing he could do, that the fire was too intense to go in after them.

I watched as the fire fighters tried to stop the flames, but there was nothing they could do. The house had burned to the ground leaving nothing but charred wood and ashes. When the firemen were able to proceed in, they found what was left of my parents in their bed. To this day, I wish I hadn't been there to see it, to watch them die like that.

I hurried up the steps to join my sister. She stood inside the doorway of her old room like she was in a trance. I don't even think she knew I was there.

"Everything okay with you?" She jumped, as if I had startled her.

"Yeah, I'm fine," she answered. "I was just thinking back on all the times I spent in this room. It feels like yesterday." I watched her wipe the tears sliding down her face. A part of me wanted to reach out to this woman I called my sister and embrace her in a hug, but my head and heart were fighting for control at the moment and I knew trying to hug her wouldn't be to my benefit. Instead, with as much sensitivity as my hug might have encompassed, I lay my hand on her shoulder.

"I'm sorry," she whispered. "I don't even know why I'm crying."

"No need to be sorry. I cried, too, before you arrived." I wrapped my arm around her, and she leaned her head on my shoulder. I don't know how long we stood there, a few minutes, maybe more. The memories of the lost years of understanding and care between sisters seemed to fill the space around us as this embrace proved that every relationship can have a second chance.

"I shouldn't have treated you the way I did back then. I...I just want you to know I'm sorry for what happened," she said.

At first, I remained silent, but I needed to let her know that I understood why. "Hey, we were kids back then; we didn't know any better," was all I could say before my throat compressed. I had tried many times to forgive her, but I wasn't ready to do that, at least not yet. I think she realized that. I guess we both needed to forgive each other before we could move on.

"Let's go get some lunch?" I suggested, changing the subject. "We can catch up on old times later." I released my hold and started down the stairs.

Standing outside, I soaked up the mid–morning sun. Closing my eyes, I took in a deep breath and cleared my mind. I had to let go of the past and move on. I hoped that I had made the right choice to move back here. Back where the events in my life had changed everything.

2

I spent the next few hectic days in the house I had lived in for eleven years, packing our belongings and getting rid of what we didn't need. As I sorted through the many miscellaneous objects I had collected over the years, I began to recognize that I had the genes of a hoarder, since it was hard to let many items go as I remembered everything about the once precious possessions. I needed to remind myself that this was a welcome change, for the better and not for the worse.

I stood in the kitchen when the movers arrived early Friday morning, then put the last of the food in a cooler and set it in my car. Glancing around one last time, I let go of this place I had called home.

A few hours later, I was standing in our new home, watching as the men unloaded the truck. My sister said she would pick Brent up from school and stop for ice cream before coming over to help me unpack.

I kept busy putting things away. I didn't even

realize it was getting dark outside. I dug in my purse for my cell phone. No messages. *They should have been here by now,* I thought. Dialing my sister's number, I waited to hear her voice as it went straight to voice mail.

"She never has her phone off," I mumbled just before I left a quick message to call me. Pacing for a few minutes without realizing it, I caught myself and went into the kitchen to finish unpacking.

I felt as if someone was watching me so I began to search the room and then looked out the window above the sink. At first it seemed someone was standing by the huge oak tree, but after I rubbed my eyes and looked again, the figure was gone.

Again, I found myself pacing from room to room waiting for my sister to call me back; by then it was seven, then eight.

I was sitting on the sofa when my phone began to ring. I sprang to my feet hoping it was Shelia.

"Hello," I answered.

"Hello, is this Miss Iris?" the man asked.

"Yes, this is she," I responded, my heart beating hard through my chest. It wasn't Sheila's voice; it was a man's.

19

"This is Officer Bates," the man said. "I'm sorry to be calling you this late, but I just got your contact information."

Panic flowed through my body like a heat wave. "What is this about?" I asked.

"I'm sorry, but I have some bad news. Shelia Larisa was in an accident. She is at Mendota Community Hospital." Tears flooded my eyes as I tried to register what he was saying. Then, I remembered she went to pick up Brent.

"Oh, God, no!" I screamed. "What about Brent? Was Brent with her?" I asked and tried to slow my breathing.

"Yes, there was a boy with her in the car," Officer Bates replied. "They are both at Mendota Community Hospital. Ma'am, do you have someone to take you to the hospital?"

"No!" I shouted, a bit louder than intended. "I'm sorry, I mean, I can drive." I grabbed my purse and was getting in the car when he asked me how long it would take for me to get to the hospital. "I'll be there in fifteen minutes," I replied. Officer Bates said he would meet me in the lobby when I got there. I hadn't been to a hospital since….

I thought back to that day all those years ago. A time way before Brent was born that I will never let myself forget.

Stop it, Deanna. You can't think like that, I told myself as I drove to the hospital. *He will be fine, he's not going to die; you have to believe that.*

Parking the car, I sprinted up the walkway to the main entrance. The sliders zipped open when I stepped through. A man approached me, and I thought it must be Officer Bates. My eyes searched the waiting room and then focused back on him.

"Miss Iris?" I nodded. "I'll take you to your son and sister. They're in the Intensive Care Unit; their conditions are not good, I am afraid."

Tears cascaded down my face. I was angry and sad all at the same time.

"Do you need to sit down, Miss Iris?" He put his arm on my shoulder and I flinched.

I was shaking. "I can't lose him," I said.

"I'm sorry, Miss Iris, but if there is anything, anything at all I can do to help, just let me know."

"Deanna," I replied.

"Sorry?"

"My name is Deanna. You can call me by my first name." I gazed up at him, his hazel eyes glistening with sympathy, yet there seemed to be something different about him when I mentioned my name. I noticed a scar on his forehead, long and thin, his short brown hair not covering it. He reminded me of someone I once knew. I imagined from his touch that he was gentle and kind, but seemed quiet and distant. I started to feel unsteady and reached for the wall to hold me up. He grabbed my arm as I was about to faint. I pulled away from him when my back was against the wall.

"I'm fine. Really, I'll be fine," I said, hoping he would believe me and leave. Instead he led me to my son's room.

"Can you tell me what happened? What caused the accident?"

"From what the State Trooper told me, a deer ran out in front of her car and he thinks she jerked the steering wheel too hard and it caused them to hit the ditch and flip over. It took a couple of hours to get them cut out of the vehicle. They are lucky to be alive, thanks to some of the other drivers that saw it happen and called it in, but...."

"But what?" I asked.

"There's something you should know before you go in."

"What more could you possibly have to tell me?"

"I overheard before I called you that your son is unconscious and your sister is in a coma."

"Coma. You mean that she won't ever wake up?"

His eyes went wide. "I didn't say that, I just wanted you to know before you went in to see your son that he may not respond to you."

I absorbed what he was saying and had to see for myself. I took in a deep breath, and swung the door open, as Officer Bates waited outside the room.

Wires hung all around my son, and a machine beeped beside his bed. An IV, pumping fluids into his body, was attached to his left arm. On his right arm, I could see only his fingers; a light blue cast hid the rest of his arm to his shoulder. I stood beside him and stroked his cheek. Tears slithered down my face as I noted that he didn't even look like my son. His face was covered with cuts and bruises; he was unrecognizable.

This morning he had left for school wearing his favorite Cubs shirt and a pair of jeans. He was so excited about living in our new home and couldn't wait to sleep in his room. He begged me to allow him to stay home from school, but I said no and that I would see him later. He tried to change my mind and said it was the last day of school and that he didn't really need to go. Now I wished I'd let him remain with me, as then he wouldn't be lying here in this bed, hurt, helpless and alone, and perhaps even dying.

I smoothed his hair, though most of it had been shaved and replaced with stitches. I kissed his forehead, feeling the warmth of his body. I whispered, "Please God, let him be okay. Don't take him from me. He's all I have, and I can't live without him."

When I came out of the room, Officer Bates was sitting with his eyes closed in the chair. I nudged his arm, and his eyes popped open.

"Sorry, I didn't mean to fall asleep," he said, yawning,

"It's okay," I replied. "It's been a long night. Can you take me to my sister now? I would like to see her." He nodded, then stood and stretched. We went down a couple of doors to where he pointed to her room.

"You don't have to stay, you know. I'll be fine. Go home and get some sleep," I said, staring into his bloodshot eyes.

"Are you sure you don't need me to stay?" he replied. "Do you have family nearby that can stay with you?" He yawned again. "Do you need me to contact your sister's husband and let him know what has happened?"

"No," I said shaking my head, in part to clear the haze of despair that was beginning to set in. "They are all I have, and as for her husband, he died after they were married four years ago." I didn't give him time to respond; I turned and pushed the door open, leaving him outside.

Standing at her bedside, I gasped. Her face was puffy and black and blue. A neck brace was wrapped around her neck, pushing up the skin on her cheeks and chin. Her left arm lay on a pillow, while the right arm was raised in a sling, both in casts. A nurse came in to check her vitals, and I asked about my sister. She began talking to me about the Glasgow Coma Scale, which was a fifteen-point test that helped a doctor assess the initial severity of a brain injury by checking a person's ability to follow directions and move their eyes and limbs. The coherence of speech also provided important clues.

I stopped the nurse a moment asking if my sister was awake when she was brought in.

The nurse said that my sister was brought in unconscious.

I had so many questions. How could my sister have been helped in any way by a test she couldn't pass when she had been brought to the hospital? How could a test to assess her coherence work when she was unable to answer their questions?

The nurse seemed as frustrated with me as I was with her. "The abilities are scored numerically. Higher scores mean milder injuries. A CT scan was run to visualize fractures and uncover evidence of bleeding in the brain or swelling."

Before she could finish I asked her if an MRI had been done.

Shaking her head as if I didn't understand hospital emergency procedure, she replied, "Doctors don't often use MRIs during emergency assessments of traumatic brain injuries because the procedure takes too long. That test can be used after the person's condition has stabilized."

The nurse told me that my sister was in a coma due to a brain injury. My attention lost focus as she started to tell me about the tissue swelling and how the doctor had inserted a probe through my sister's skull to monitor the pressure. After all that information, the nurse ended the conversation with, "Your sister was lucky to have survived at all."

I sat in a chair next to Sheila's bed and touched her fingers that lay motionless on the sheet. I don't know how long I sat there staring at her, praying she would wake up, and I wanted so much to tell her that I would forgive her. I wished I knew why it was so difficult to talk to her. To tell her everything I felt inside, like sisters should.

3

I awoke in the middle of the night to the odd sounds of Brent's mechanical ventilator, not sure how long I'd been asleep. Brent didn't stir; he just lay there, sleeping. I had forgotten my watch at home so I dug in my purse and pulled out my cell phone. It was a little past three in the morning. Standing, I stretched, never taking my eyes off him. I kissed him on the forehead; then I left.

I needed coffee, something to keep me awake. A petite blonde nurse at the desk suggested I go home and sleep, that there was nothing I could do, and if anything changed, she would call me. I scribbled down my cell phone number and handed it to her. I asked the nurse if they could move my sister into the same room with my son, but she said I would have to wait on that until I talked to their doctor in the morning.

Once in the elevator, with my index finger hovering over what button to push, I decided the nurse was right, that I would be no good to them if I were exhausted. Besides, I could use a shower and clean clothes.

The house was dark when I arrived. Past the stairs, I glanced down the hall to my old room, where Brent would be sleeping, and a thought came across my mind. Brent hadn't had a chance to sleep in his new bedroom. I turned and made my way down the hall. I opened the door to the bedroom and stretched out; soaking in his scent from the blanket I had spread over his bed yesterday. I began to cry just like I did many years ago in this same room. Wishing the pain would go away.

Birds were singing when I opened my eyes. A dry crust had formed on my eyes; I headed into the bathroom and washed my face. Looking into the mirror, I saw my hair flat on one side. I took a long hard look, just like I used to do when I was young, and studied every detail of my image. *When did I become so old?* I asked myself, knowing that I had lived for yesterday and never today. I wished Brice were with me now, he would know what to do.

Closing my eyes, I remembered everything that we said just a few days ago. I was upstairs packing when he came over. I offered him something to drink and we sat out on the patio. I sensed that he had something to discuss, but he didn't know how to start so I spoke first.

"What's on your mind, Brice?" His eyes looked over at me from across the table, then away.

"Deanna, I think you know how I feel about you and Brent. I wish you weren't moving so far away. I just wish…." His voice trailed off. "I just wish you would love me back. You're not telling me something, and I want you to know that you can trust me. Whatever it is, I will always be there for you to lean on. You can tell me anything, anything at all. I have known you and loved you for nine years." I could see that he was nervous; his hand was shaking as he tried to hold the glass and so he set it down.

I had no intention of telling him how much I loved him. I felt, even though the emotions were there, it was better that we went our separate ways as if we had never met. Although that wasn't what I really wanted; to be honest, I didn't know what I wanted. Looking at this man who had been both friend and confidant, I realized I hadn't made the time to decide with whom I wanted to spend my life. Besides, I had Brent to consider.

When I first met Brice, I would watch him from the family room window when he would be out in his yard mowing or raking leaves. My eyes would take in every detail of his body, especially when he had his shirt off. I don't think he knew I was watching; at least he never gave any indication. When I mustered the nerve to introduce myself, we became inseparable, but only as friends. After my last relationship, I couldn't allow myself anything but that. Yet I could see he wanted more from me.

"Brice, please. Please don't do this now." I was almost begging. "We have been such great friends all these years, and I don't want to lose that."

"Friends, huh! Well, I can't keep living like this, Deanna. It's too hard. I need to know how you feel about us. Is there even the possibility of an 'us'?" His voice rose as his accent deepened. "I love you and want to marry you."

I gave a nervous smile back at him, hoping he wouldn't see the shock on my face. I needed to be strong and end it with him. Though in all honesty, I didn't want to hurt him. I never meant to hurt him.

"Brice, I wish I could tell you what is going on inside, but I'm sorry, I can't, not yet. I wish to stay friends, nothing else." I could see the pain in his eyes, but I couldn't take back what I had just said, not now. My heart was heavy as I asked myself why I couldn't open up to this wonderful man and tell him why I was so afraid. I couldn't bring myself to admit that I feared if he knew what happened so long ago that he wouldn't love me or want to be with me. I didn't want to lose him, but what else could I do or say to make him understand?

"Then I guess this is good-bye." He said nothing more, stood up and left. I heard the front door close on his way out. The thought was there, how I could stop him before he reached the door, but I was paralyzed by my own indecisiveness. Tears trickled down my face. I didn't even wipe them away. I allowed myself to weep, while thinking of all the moments Brice and I had spent together. Never had I wanted to kick myself more than I did now.

God, I missed his arms around me, hugging me, comforting me. My heart ached, knowing I had let him go and that he would move on with his life, without me. I should have said I loved him, but didn't. I wondered if maybe, just maybe, he would have stood by me and loved me no matter what had happened when I was young. Maybe my therapist was right; I should forgive myself first, then I would be able to let someone else in and heal. But there was always that what if part, like what if he couldn't handle what happened? What if he couldn't stand to touch me anymore, knowing what was done to me?

After I showered and dressed, I found a duffle bag and shoved a change of clothes in it for Brent and other things he would need when he woke up, if he woke up. I slipped on my watch and unplugged my cell from its charger and hurried out the door, locking it behind me.

Slipping past the nurse's station, I entered my son's room. I set his belongings in the cabinet across from the bed, and then took a seat beside him. Opening the book I had brought with me, I began to read aloud. It was Brent's favorite story, one that I had read to him since he was a baby. He would have me read it to him over and over, until I knew it by heart. When he was able to walk, he would wobble into my office, and I would watch from the corner of my eye as he approached my desk, the book clutched tight under his tiny arm, and then he would lay it down in front of me. It always brought a smile to my face. I would stop what I was doing and scoop him up in my arms and read him the story of *Where the Wild Things Are*.

I didn't know anyone had entered the room, until I heard the door click shut. Turning, I saw a young woman standing near the door. I assumed she was a doctor by the long white coat she was wearing, but she didn't look old enough to be a doctor.

"I love that story," the doctor said while I wondered who she was. "My mom used to read it to me when I was a baby."

I didn't reply; in fact, I couldn't stop looking at her. There was something drawing me toward her. Her eyes. Her face. Her long dark hair. "I'm sorry; what did you say?"

"I loved that story when I was young."

"It's a good story," I replied, closing the book.

"I'm Dr. Kimberly Sheldon, by the way. I will be the doctor in charge of your son's care while he is here in the hospital. We are going to be taking your son for a CT scan here in a few minutes; you're more than welcome to come along."

"I'll stay here and visit with my sister."

"Is your sister a patient, too?"

"Yes." I could hear the sadness in my voice as the words tumbled out. "She is in Intensive Care, her name is Shelia Larisa."

"Oh, I'm so sorry," she replied, a look of recognition crossing her face. "I am aware of your situation. One of the critical care nurses took your request to the charge nurse who then notified me."

"Yes," I answered, then asked for her decision about whether to move my sister into Brent's room.

"I can arrange that after his tests." Dr. Sheldon glided to the other side of the bed and checked the monitor. Her eyes were on me as I stared at her, as if she wanted to say something to me but didn't know how. Every detail of her face struck me as if I had seen her before, but couldn't put my finger on when.

35

Shaking the thoughts from my head, I stared back
down at my son, who showed no signs of waking up.

"Do you think he will come back to me?" I
asked.

"He did suffer a traumatic head injury, but I
have hopes that he will pull through. We are going to
check his brain for any enlargement, and that should
tell us more. If the swelling is going down, then he
should become conscious within a few days," she
replied. I could feel her eyes again on me, studying my
reaction.

"That is good news, right? I can't lose him,
Doctor, he's all I have. My life would be empty
without him."

"We'll know more once we examine the results.
Deanna, your son is in good hands. I promise you that."
Dr. Sheldon reached over and patted my hand.

"What about my sister, Shelia? Is she suffering
from the same problem? Is her brain swollen, too?" I
asked, hoping for a different response.

"Shelia's head collided with the roof of the car
and the driver's side window, but we were able to stop
the bleeding in her brain caused by the accident. We

are observing her and will run more tests. I have those scheduled for later today, after Brent's." I watched as she jotted notes into his chart, and then hung it at the end of the bed. I waited for her to leave before reading what she had written.

"It is quite understandable that the patient's mother is on edge due to his condition. Please inform me of any adverse changes in her behavior towards the staff. Should set up an appointment with hospital psychologist, if behavior persists."

"Of course, I'm emotional," I said out loud. "My son is unconscious and my sister is in a coma and there's nothing I can do but pray and wait for them to come out of it." I buried my face in my hands and wept.

4

I looked at my watch. An hour had passed since they wheeled Brent away for tests, and I began to wonder what was taking so long. I walked over to the nurse's station and asked a redheaded woman, who was overweight, where my son was now.

"They were having problems with the machine," she replied. "But I'll call down and ask how the tests are going." I nodded and turned away, heading back to Shelia's room.

A nurse I hadn't seen before was examining her. She didn't seem to notice me standing near the door. So I moved to the side of the bed and sat down. The nurse looked over and smiled at me. She had perfect straight teeth that people only dream of, and her dark brown eyes sparkled in the fluorescent light that accented her brown shoulder–length hair.

I encased my fingers around my sister's hand and squeezed. This accident in a matter of minutes changed my life, flipping my world upside down and leaving me reeling. My everyday life had come to an abrupt halt, as I had to come to terms with the uncertainty of not knowing whether these people I loved would survive or how much they would change if they did.

I had become lost in my thoughts.

What woke me from my trance was when Shelia moved her hand in mine. I thought my heart was going to come bolting out of me. I glanced at her lying there, smiling up at me. She was awake. That's all that mattered right then and there, that she was awake. I smiled at her, but what she said next felt like someone punched me in the stomach.

"Hi, Mom," she said, clear as a bell. I resembled our mother, as if we were twins, but she had died ten years ago.

"Shelia, it's me, Deanna." I could feel my facial expression softening as I stared at her. Moving closer, so the light would be out of my face, I waited for her to see who I was and not who she thought I was.

"Deanna. Deanna's only a kid. You don't look like a kid."

I glanced over at the nurse. "What is wrong with her?" I asked. "Why does she not know me?"

"It's the swelling in her brain. Once it goes down, she may remember recent events but I will make a note of it and talk to the doctor. I'm sure she'll be fine."

"Why does everyone say that?" I said, my voice rising. Remembering what the doctor had written, I tried to hold back, but I couldn't control myself, and the words just slipped out and kept coming.

"How do you know? Can you tell the future? By the way things look to me it's not fine! My boy is in another room, maybe dying, and my sister thinks I'm our mother. She doesn't recognize me, and we just saw each other a few days ago." I sat down in the chair and tried to get a grip, taking those calming breaths in through my nose and out through my mouth, just as my therapist told me to do.

"I'm sorry, really I am, but this is expected after the head trauma she suffered. After the swelling goes down, memories will come back to her, and she will know who you are. If you would like, I could send the doctor in to see you and go over this to help you understand the condition better," the nurse suggested.

I didn't even look up at her; I just nodded my

head and closed my eyes, continuing to calm myself. The nurse left a few seconds later, and my sister had fallen back into a deep sleep as if she had never been awake. My head was spinning. I moved back to my old house, and this happened. It seemed that I wasn't supposed to live in this town where I grew up. I thought it would be a new beginning for us, but if we hadn't moved my son and my sister wouldn't be in this predicament. It was like the past was coming back to haunt me all over again. I wished it would go away. I just wanted to forget what happened.

I just wanted to move on.

I went to the cafeteria for coffee and something to eat, though I wasn't hungry. I knew I should eat because I needed to keep my strength up. When I returned to Intensive Care, Brent was back in his room.

I sat next to him combing my fingers through his hair. He loved it when I did that to him. I remembered sitting next to him in our old house. He had been sick with the flu. The doctor said it was an intestinal virus and would pass in a few days to a week. That was the longest week ever. I couldn't get any food into his body without him vomiting it up. I brought my laptop into his room and wrote while he slept, unable to bring myself to leave his side.

The door was flung open, and the redheaded nurse from the desk entered. She and another nurse were bringing my sister in and setting up an area next to Brent. *Now I can be with both of them,* I thought. Listening to the machines beep, I pulled out the book I was reading earlier and began where I left off.

I must have dozed off because I was awakened by the sound of an alarm. I lay my hand on my chest as if trying to keep my heart from leaping out of me. The door burst open, and four nurses brought in a crash cart next to my son's bed. No! I tried to say, but the words were stuck in my throat and wouldn't escape. I stood frozen in place, and then one of the nurses grabbed my arms, shaking me from a state of shock.

"Deanna, I'm sorry, but you'll have to leave," I heard her say, but I couldn't move. She wrapped her arms around my shoulders and escorted me out into the hallway. There I stood wondering what was happening to my son. I turned to go back in, but the nurse standing near the doorway said no, not yet.

"You'll have to wait out here until they're done with him," she said in a gentle voice.

"I need to be with him. Please," I begged, tears sliding down my face. "Please don't let him die. He's my son, and I need him. Please." I covered my face with my hands and wept. The nurse led me to a private lounge down the hall. We both sat, waiting for word about Brent. My vision blurred several times as I tried to register what she was saying.

A few moments later Dr. Sheldon entered the room. "Deanna, your son is in stable condition. His heart did stop, but we were able to bring him back. We will have to keep a closer eye on him. I have scheduled more tests for him, just to make sure there is no blockage around his heart."

"Can I go see him now?" I asked, swiping at the tears.

"It's best to wait until they finish running the tests. They're doing that as we speak," she replied. Taking a seat next to me, she touched my hand. I felt her squeeze my fingers. I looked up at her. Her eyes were a deep blue, with a locket of her hair hanging along her high cheekbones. She reminded me of someone I knew long ago, but couldn't quite put my finger on it. I sobbed and then turned away. That's when it came to me who she resembled. I took another look at her, a good hard look. I don't know why I didn't see it before, but now, now I knew. Those eyes gave her away. The same blue eyes that have haunted me every night since I was fourteen.

5

I wanted to believe it was all a dream. No way was she my baby. My baby girl died twenty-six years ago. But what if she didn't die? What if it was all a lie? I needed to know what happened back then. Making my way to the elevator, I rode down to the lobby and then left the hospital.

The sun was just coming up on the horizon. Twisting the watch on my wrist to see what time it was, I couldn't believe that a whole day had gone by, that I had slept through the night. I prayed that my son would be fine until I got back.

I climbed into my car and drove out of the parking lot. Turning left at the light, I went down Thirteenth Avenue. Four more blocks and I would be there, and might find the confirmation I needed. I turned onto Destiny Lane that led through the main entrance of Holy Cross Cemetery, and slowed my car down to a crawl, letting it creep down the gravel road. I stopped in front of an old decrepit building.

Stepping out of my car, I felt the weight of the world press down upon my shoulders as I glanced around. I saw the old maple tree that had I chosen so many years ago. The last time I could remember seeing the tree it was a sapling. It was much larger now. It stood tall with many branches and leaves, shading my daughter while she lay in her final resting place. The sun was playing peek-a-boo with a cloud as a gust of wind tousled my hair and then the place became still.

I looked back at the shack. I gave myself a few moments to think before I went up the brick path and knocked on the door. I could hear floorboards creaking inside, as steps came towards me. The door swung open, and a tall slim elderly man with white hair stared down at me.

"Deanna, is that you, girl?" he grumbled with a shallow voice. I was astonished that he had remembered me from all those years ago. After we had moved, I would take a train here to visit her and to see him. He was the only person I could talk to without feeling judged. I just wished I had stayed in contact with him after I finished school.

"Yes, it's me, Deanna," I replied.

"Come in, come in. What brings you to this neck of the woods, my girl?" He hadn't called me his girl since…since I was eighteen. "Hello, Mr. Vashon. It has been a long time, hasn't it?"

"Please, call me Hank." He motioned with his hand to a flower–patterned sofa near a window. I had never been in his home, though I honestly didn't believe when I was young that someone actually lived in what I had always thought was a crumbling old structure. We always sat outside or strolled around the cemetery.

A little light was shining through the window, but I was still able to get a good look around. My eyes took time adjusting to the darkness, but from what I could see, a mini kitchen with a small wooden table and a single chair were on the other side from where I stood. Against the other wall was a cot, which I assumed was his bed. I felt sad to think that he lived alone, and I wondered if I would one day have a life like that. Closing my eyes and shaking my head, I walked over to the sofa and took a seat.

"How have you been, Hank?" I asked, soaking in his kindness.

"I'm doing well. Hanging in there, you know. Been keeping busy when I can, so many things to look after in this cemetery. Trimming the lawn, pulling weeds, and making sure the flowers stay watered. But you don't want to hear about that, do you, girl? I don't think you came here to ask about me?" His eyes sparkled as if they were smiling at me.

"Well, I did come to ask a question, but I don't want to bother you." I hoped I didn't sound rude; I didn't want him to think I didn't care how he was doing. Of course, I cared; he was there for me when I buried my daughter.

"My girl, you don't bother me. I always have time to talk with you." He scratched his chin with his long wiry fingers then let his hand fall to his lap. He looked so tired and weak.

"I…I was hoping you could help me with something," I said. I could feel myself trembling. The reason I came scared the life out of me. But I just had to know. "Do you remember when I was here last, with my mother?"

"Yes, yes, I do. I'm so sorry to hear what happened to them."

48

"Thank you," I said, with a grin that I was sure looked more like a grimace.

"What is it that you want to know?"

"Something has happened that makes me think…." *Come on, you can do this,* I told myself. *Just say it. Tell him why you came.* I cleared my throat and started once more. "I need for you to dig up my daughter's grave." There, I said it. I took in a deep breath and tried to relax, looking into his face, studying it. The blood had drained from his cheeks, giving him the pale complexion of a corpse.

He stood and paced the floor then stopped beside the chair. I could see the tension in his jaw before he began to speak. "Deanna, why would you want to do that? What has happened that makes you want to disturb her grave? Your child is with God now. Let her rest in peace."

"I have this feeling inside me that she may still be alive. That maybe she never died. I don't know how I know, I just do, and it would help if you could do this for me. If I could just get a look inside her casket, then I'll know, and I can put this to rest. Please, Hank, I just can't go through this again. I have to know that she is

49

in that casket. That we did bury her all those years ago."
I didn't want him to ask me any more questions. I
wanted him to say yes, and for that to be the end of it,
but I had a feeling it wouldn't be that simple. He must
have thought I was nuts. How many people want to dig
up a loved one, just to see if they really died? My
therapist would have me committed if she knew about
this.

"I don't know if I can do that for you. You
buried her and then moved away, and except for the
few times that you visited, you haven't been back since.
Now you are begging me to dig her up as if she was
just put in the ground yesterday." He paced the floor
again, but this time I could see he was wringing his
hands in torment as if I were asking him to kill
someone.

He stopped and sat down in front of me, "I
have only one question for you, and a few words to say,
but this doesn't mean I am agreeing to this…this
ungodly request you have thrown into my lap.

"Okay. Sounds fair." I crossed my fingers
under my purse.

"You say you have a feeling that she is alive,

but my question is: Didn't you see her one last time before we buried her?" His question puzzled me, since I'd never thought about that. I did see her lying in the casket that my mother and I picked out for her. Wearing a pink frilly dress that I had bought for her before she was born. It was only for a moment that I saw her lying there motionless. My father had told my mother it would be best if I didn't see my baby, so they closed the casket the moment I walked in.

"Yes, I did, but I have feelings stirring inside that tell me to take another look, and then I can put it to rest. I'll swear to it. I'm sorry for asking you this, but please, please, do this for me. I wouldn't be asking if I didn't suspect she was alive." Sweat beaded on my forehead, and I felt hot all over. My stomach was churning. I didn't know what I would do if he said no. He couldn't say no, I was his girl. Not his daughter, I understood, but someone he connected with years ago like I was his daughter.

"My girl," he said, the look on his face worrying me. "To exhume a body there are many laws that need to be enforced. Have you applied for the appropriate exhumation license?"

"Um, no," I said my heart sinking into my gut. "I just wanted to set my mind at ease. Please, isn't there anything you can do?"

"I hate to tell you this, my girl, but under current law, courts do not allow exhumation unless there are substantial and compelling reasons to do so."

"I have substantial and compelling reasons," I said, raising my voice. "I know about the laws of exhumation, but I guess I was hoping you could overlook that, and help a friend out," I pleaded.

Holding up three fingers, Hank began explaining the rules of exhumation, but my heart didn't care about the rules or laws. "Three general principles govern the law of disinterment in the United States." He lowered two fingers, leaving the index finger pointing up. "First, it is presumed that a 'decently buried' body should remain undisturbed where it was placed unless good reason is given not to do so."

"Good reason," I said placing my hand on my chest. "I have a very good reason."

Raising his middle finger next to his index finger, Hank kept talking as though I hadn't spoken. "Second, disinterment is considered the private concern of the immediate family and the cemetery."

"I am the only immediate family my daughter has. And I don't care what the cemetery has to say. This cemetery didn't give my daughter life. I did. The only part this place played in her life was to give my daughter an eternal place to rest." I could hear in my tone my increasing anger.

He still wasn't listening to me as he raised a third finger and continued talking about close relatives and disagreements about exhumation.

Shaking my head, I argued, "There won't be a disagreement among the close relatives. I am her closest relative. I am her mother."

Without fail he kept talking about unauthorized disturbance of a grave, criminal offense and Class Three felony, all about which I didn't really care to hear.

"We aren't going to, how did you put it? Willfully destroy anything or damage her remains." Whatever was holding back my tears was going to break loose. "I would never think of doing such a thing."

"I'm not done, my girl. If you are serious about

this, then you need to know what you are asking of me."

"So get to the brass tacks. You're telling me no." I felt the petulant child within me coming forward. I felt yet again that I wasn't going to get my way, and another wish would be held just an arm's length away from me.

"Let me think about it, Deanna, and I will give you a call. You do know what you're asking of me, don't you?"

"Yes, I do, and it breaks my heart to ask this of you. My baby girl has been at peace, and I should feel ashamed of myself, but I need to know. A new development has come up and it's eating at me. I can't help but think what if she hadn't died, that it was set-up in some way, like, like someone planned all of this." Hank handed me a handkerchief from his flannel shirt pocket, and I wiped the sweat from my eyes and forehead. The temperature in the room seemed to be accelerating. I fanned my shirt against my chest and asked for a glass of water. Hank returned with a gray demitasse, and I guzzled it down, handing it back to him; he refilled it from a pitcher sitting on the counter.

"Deanna, it's been twenty-six years since she was buried. Do you think there will be anything left of her?"

"I don't know, I didn't think about that. One second I saw her and the next I was racing here. I'm sorry, you must think I'm crazy, but I assure you I am fine, Hank. My son and I just moved back into the house my parents once owned, and when I was home unpacking, I got a call. My sister, Shelia, had persuaded me to let her pick up my son from school, but they never made it to the house. They were in an accident and are in critical condition at Mendota Community Hospital. The only reason I am bringing this up is because of their doctor."

"Shelia was in an accident?"

"Yes, Officer Bates told me that a deer crossing caused the accident. It must have been bad for her to hit her head and end up in a coma."

"I see."

Something didn't seem right about him. He seemed more concerned about my sister than Brent, or maybe I just didn't notice it before, but I could tell his attitude was different.

"And what does the doctor have to do with all of this?" A baffled look crossed his face as I finished telling him about her. "She has his eyes, Hank. The same blue eyes that made me fall in love with him, the same eyes that still haunt me. You know what I'm talking about; you were the one I confided in back then. The only one." We sat in silence for what seemed like an eternity before he spoke.

"Deanna, my girl. There are some truths I am certain about, and one of them is that your baby girl can't be alive. It could just be coincidence that the doctor resembles your daughter's father. But, if this is what you want, then—" He stopped mid-sentence as though still thinking.

"Please, Hank," I said, trying not to sound like I was begging. "We can do this. But I don't want to get you into any legal trouble."

"Not just legal trouble, my girl," he said. "I rely on this job. It pays my bills and puts a roof over my head. I know it might not seem like much to you, but to me it is everything."

"I would never ask you if this wasn't important to me." The words tumbled from my lips, although I knew I sounded like a person thinking only of herself. "There has to be a way."

"There might be one way."

He had my attention.

"Statutes are not directed against cemetery authorities who wish to change the place of burial and who are authorized to do so."

"And that means?" I asked.

"I will do it for you. But I am not the cemetery authority. You have to give me a few days to talk to him. If it's her in that casket, will you promise me you will let this go and move on with your life? Your son needs you more than ever now, and your sister, too." He cleared his throat. I could see that he was getting tired as his eyes were half closed. "I am so sorry about your boy, but Deanna, this could be a sign that you need to live your life and leave the past in the past where it belongs. You can't worry about getting hurt, and living in the past won't heal you. I know you will not forget her, but you must move on and start living your life before it's over. Don't end up like me, old and alone."

She's not forgotten, that's for certain, I thought to myself before I spoke. "I promise, Hank." We hugged good-bye, and he walked me to the door.

"Give me a few days," he said.

I nodded and went out the door, hearing it click shut behind me. Before opening the door to my car, I looked over at the tree one last time.

6

The sliders opened, and I stepped through the entrance into Intensive Care. One nurse was busy filing and doing other tasks while several others were chirping among themselves as I walked by. Two of the ladies looked over at me, and then went back to their conversation. Part of me thought they were talking about me, but I didn't care. I just wanted to see my son.

I reached for the handle to open the door and felt a tap on my shoulder. I jumped at the touch.

"Sorry, Miss Iris, I didn't mean to startle you," the voice said.

Turning towards her, I glanced up at Dr. Sheldon's face then away. "That's okay. Just a little on edge is all. Is there something wrong?" I asked.

"No, I just wanted to give you an update before checking on my other patients. Brent is doing much better, and there is no blockage around his heart. All the tests came back negative. Crashes are all different, and there are heaps of different factors that can affect the degree of injuries suffered by people in a vehicle."

I began to notice the compassion in her voice as she talked about my son. "As you are already aware, when Brent first came in, his breathing was impaired, and he exhibited no purposeful movements. Patients sometimes lack awareness and wakefulness. He was not responsive to any external stimuli or pain. Most victims in a rollover hit the door and/or the roof of the vehicle. Many of Brent's injuries may have been caused by his seatbelt pulling him in one direction while his body was rotating toward the door. Now, as everyone understands, a seatbelt doesn't stop the head from moving, so it is the most vulnerable part of the body. From Brent's injuries, I believe both scenarios occurred. His head not only hit the passenger door, but also the roof. There is no way of knowing what a body goes through during an auto accident. It's merely a matter of waiting. It can take days, even weeks for injuries to surface, and then as symptoms appear, we can meet the victim's medical needs."

"Okay, so it's not looking better? Is that what you are saying?"

"When Brent was brought in, we treated his open wounds and established proper breathing and blood flow to the brain. Yesterday, your son may have had a moment of diminished cardiac output due to tension, unless you know of any underlying medical problems or other conditions."

"No, he has always been a healthy boy," I said, trying not to stare at her.

"What you need to remember is that Brent's body has been through a traumatic experience. To reduce intracranial pressure I prescribed medication. The swelling and bruising around his brain have diminished. Because there is no cure, I feel the need to tell you treatment options are limited to preventing further damage, treating underlying causes, and maintaining proper blood flow and nutrition."

As she spoke, I began to understand that my family had been matched with the perfect doctor. I had over the years met doctors who only shared information in a clinical business-like manner, and made me believe my knowledge was inferior to theirs. But Dr. Sheldon had an excellent bedside manner. The way she was speaking to me made me feel more like a friend than a business client. She may not have been a perfect match for other people who wouldn't appreciate her emotional approach. She explained conditions that she didn't need to explain, but I could tell that she wanted to set my mind at ease.

"What you need to remember is a patient's chance of recovery is dependent on the severity of the injury sustained and the amount of time spent in an unconscious state."

"And how long do you think that will be with my son?" I asked.

"To help determine the chance of regaining consciousness, doctors…." Dr. Sheldon paused and smiled. It was a radiant smile; just like the smile I could picture my daughter having. The way her lips curved reminded me of my baby. "Doctors classify a traumatic brain injury into one of six abnormal conscious states: stupor, coma, vegetative state, persistent vegetative state, locked-in syndrome, and brain dead." I felt myself gasp at the words, "brain dead." "Brent will be in the stupor state when he wakes. And he will awaken. He may be in a dream state for some time. There is no medical reason for me to believe he will slip into any of the other states. However, it depends on the person and their will to live."

"You don't know my son, but he is a strong and willful young man," I said, almost reaching out and patting her hand before stopping myself.

"If that is the case, I'm quite sure that he will be awaking soon. Then we can proceed from there. I do have some good news for you. Currently, Brent is breathing on his own. We were able to take him off his ventilator." I digested every word she was saying, and I smiled.

"This is great news!" I shouted, then noticed everyone gawking at me. I glanced at the doctor and motioned for her to come into my son's room with me. She closed the door behind her, and we sat down near the window.

"Do you want to talk about your sister?" she asked. "The nurse told me what happened the other day when she woke up. A person in a coma does not always lie still or quiet. Sometimes a person can talk or perform other functions that appear to be conscious acts, but are not. According to the scans that we took of her brain, they showed no signs of lacerations or hemorrhaging since the last time, but there was still an extreme amount of swelling and bruising. I will be doing tests every other day, unless something else should occur. The confusion that she had is common in cases like hers, but I have great expectations that she'll get better. Once her swelling goes down, she should come out of the coma, but until then we will have to wait and see."

I watched her lips moving as she talked about my sister and soaked in her voice and memorized the features on her face. What if this was my baby all grown up sitting here in front of me? Her traits were so similar to mine, like the high cheekbones and long, thick black hair. Sure, it could just be a coincidence. But I could feel the connection deep inside me that she was my daughter.

I wanted to ask her so many questions, but this was neither the time nor the place to talk about personal details. We didn't know each other, but I reminded myself that everyone needs to talk. As soon as the words entered my mind, I thought of Brice. He was there for me whenever I needed him and even when I didn't. He never pushed.

"Well, I better get back to work. Is there anything else you would like to know that has to do with your son or sister?"

"No," I said. Just like that, I had to watch this woman whom I felt an overwhelming attachment to walk away from me as she left the room.

I took a seat alongside my son, and lowered his bed rail. I lay my head next to his chest and closed my eyes, replaying my conversation with Hank.

I jolted upright and realized that I must have dozed off for a while. I squinted at my son then rubbed my eyes. Nothing was different. He still lay peacefully in his bed.

From the corner of my eye, I caught a glimpse of the book I was reading earlier to him, and I remembered that when my daughter died, I had the mortician put the same book in her casket.

7

I had spent all night listening to the beeping of their monitors and couldn't fall back to sleep. All I thought about was my meeting with Hank and looking into my daughter's casket and learning the truth. What would I do if she were alive? I'd missed so much of her life.

I closed my eyes and thought about the last time I had seen Levin and what he had done to me.

The night he took everything good about me away.

I shivered from the thoughts that remained embedded in my head. After what he did, I tried twice to end my life. The first time, I swallowed half a bottle of Excedrin. I hadn't eaten in days and wasn't sleeping. I was in such despair that I went into my parents' bathroom and searched their medicine cabinet, but all I found was the Excedrin, no sleeping pills, nothing that would work better than aspirin.

I opened the bottle and poured the pills into my

palm. I locked myself in my room. Holding a glass of water, I tilted my head back and tossed in a handful of capsules with no hesitation, followed by a few swallows of the water. And waited for death to come. The only thing I experienced was my legs sort of went numb. Like they wanted to buckle out from under me. I sat on the edge of my bed then lay back. The room was spinning, and my stomach ached. I thought, *here I go. I'm going to die now.*

Lying on my side, I closed my eyes. I guess it must have been a couple of hours or so later when I pushed myself upright and stood. My head wasn't swimming, and my legs weren't paralyzed.

I didn't die.

I knew I was depressed but didn't know how to fix it. There was no way I was going to let my parents know that I wanted to end it, that I wasn't cut out for this world. The one truth I always told myself was: I didn't ask to be born.

Although I'd never thought about death, until that day.

I think back on the exact time I met him. I was hanging out with some of my girlfriends at a party and he was standing by the bonfire drinking a bottle of Bud Light. My friends persuaded me to go talk to him. I accepted their dare and strode over to him. He was tall with short brown hair that feathered on the sides. He was so handsome. His voice was manly, not like the boys at school. I think that's the one attribute that attracted me most to him. I introduced myself, and one thing led to another. We dated for over a month, well, not actually dated. He was much older than I was, and God forbid my parents found out about him. I had to sneak out on the nights we spent together, after my parents went to sleep.

It was a beautiful evening, the moon lit up the sky that was midnight blue with millions of scattered stars. We were sitting on a blanket that he took from his car, a 1975 Chevy Nova. He'd had it repainted apple red, with matching interior. I only knew that because he couldn't stop talking about all the work he put into it.

We were listening to the crickets and bullfrogs. Once in a while a soft breeze teased my hair. It was a great night until…

Levin went back to the car grabbing a beer for

not only him, but also for me. When he came back to the blanket he had opened both bottles, handing me one. I didn't care much for the taste of the beer, but since he had given it to me I didn't want to upset him by not drinking it, so I sipped at it while he made fun of me for being a "light weight." Giving in to his pressure I started taking large gulps. By the end of my second beer, I started feeling dizzy. I noticed my heart rate slowed while my heart would race when he and I were together. I began to feel drowsy and a little nauseous, which I explained to Levin. My eyesight became blurry, and then it was hard to keep my eyes open, they felt heavy as lead. He told me to lie down. I'm not sure how much time had passed, but the next thing I knew my hands were being held down and my skirt was forced up and my panties were ripped off.

I tried to fight him, but not only was he much stronger than I, but I was weak. When I tried to scream, he put his hand over my mouth to quiet me. He didn't want anyone to hear me and come looking.

Not a moment goes by that I don't remember the pain I felt that night, from when he thrust himself inside me. His words were still crisp in my mind. "You want this, Deanna," he said. "You were asking for this."

After he was done, he let go of my hands and left me lying there. I was curled up in a fetus position, crying. I still wasn't able to see clearly, but in time I fixed my clothes. Levin helped me to my feet and opened the car door, placing me inside. I wasn't sure, but could swear that he had blood on his forehead, which could mean I hit him hard, but couldn't remember doing it. He never said a word to me on the ride home, nor did I to him. I hugged the car door until he stopped the car a few doors down from where I lived. I just wanted to get out of the vehicle and never see him again.

He dropped me off at the corner near my parents' house, just like he always did when I would sneak out to be with him. From there, I waddled down the sidewalk to the safety of my home. It hurt to walk, to move my legs. My abdominal wall was on fire and sharp agonizing pain struck at me like lightning on a stormy night. I had to be quiet getting into the house, so I wouldn't wake up my parents. All I wanted to do was crawl into my bed and die.

After a week went by it didn't burn to pee any longer. I never said a word to my friends or my family about that night, well, until…

Until seven weeks later when I realized my period never came. Most would say that would be the first sign of pregnancy, but I had irregular menstruations. Sometimes I would go months without having one, and then there were times it would come every couple of weeks.

For several weeks, I was vomiting the moment I stepped out of bed and smelled my mother's cooked breakfast. I wanted to go to my sister, but I just couldn't. I knew she would tell mom and dad what had happened to me, but when I noticed my belly growing, I had to do something. I had to tell them what happened that dreadful night. That's when we had to move from our house to somewhere new. My father was well known in the community. Not only was he on the city council, he was also the school principal.

She was born a little under six months, a preemie.

My father had chosen the doctor to deliver my baby and the hospital where she would be born. When

71

we arrived at the building it looked more like a doctor's office than a hospital. As we got inside the interior had the look of a small hospital, private maybe.

I was turning fifteen the day my daughter was born. My mom stood by me through the whole ordeal. My dad and sister refused to believe I was pregnant, or had been raped, for that matter. Around the house, I stayed in my room. It was better than getting stared at as if I had been sent here by the devil and I was carrying his child. One time my mother was out of the house and I was left there with them. I was in the kitchen getting something to eat and my dad and sister came into the room, pushing me into a corner.

"You're such a slut!" my sister had said. And my father was standing beside her laughing and agreeing with her. He must have been watching my eyes because he somehow knew what I was thinking.

"Don't be looking for your mother, she isn't here to save you, you whore! And I wouldn't go telling her when she gets home, or I will make sure you never have a baby, again." I stood there huddled in the corner with my arms cradling my belly and fighting back the tears, praying for them to leave the room. When they left I scurried to my room, locking the door behind me.

I still have the photo my mom took of me holding her in my arms.

The memories rushed back as I remembered holding my newborn daughter for the first time. I marveled at her eyelashes, and counted every finger and toe, twice. After the drama of her arrival at just twenty-three weeks, I knew I had a little fighter in my arms. She weighed in at a mere one pound, but I also knew our connection was instantaneous.

We were mother and daughter.

Twenty-seven minutes later, a nurse came into my room, and despite my desperate pleas for her to leave my daughter in my arms a while longer, I had to watch as she walked out of the room carrying not only my daughter, but my heart in her hands. I never thought I could love someone as much as I loved her.

I was left waiting for what seemed like forever before the door to my room opened and I sat up quickly waiting for my daughter to be placed back in my arms. Instead the doctor who had delivered my daughter came into my room with my mother trailing behind him.

That is when I was told…

My heart stopped and the tears streamed down my cheeks. The sound of the doctor's voice seemed to be coming to me from a tin can telephone. "Your daughter stopped breathing and there was nothing we could do for her. I'm sorry for your loss."

My mouth was gaping, the teenage anger growing inside me. That mother instinct I had heard about took me by surprise as at the age of fifteen the words tumbled effortless from my lips. "You put her into my arms. You let me hold her." I lifted my arms as though I was still holding her while she was wrapped in a blanket. "You placed her in my arms. She was breathing. I heard her cry. She was wiggling around. I felt her moving the way she moved inside me. When I held her with her little head lying on my shoulder I could feel her breathe on my neck."

"Deanna," my mother whispered, "they did everything they could. She was just too little and had complications."

All these years later I think back to those questions I should have asked.

Why had the medical staff handed her to me?

Was it for me to get a few minutes to say good-bye? Where was the incubator? I was certain I had felt my daughter move, and had felt her tiny breaths. If I would have seen the doctors fight in any way for my daughter then admit there was no more they could do, that would have left me with different feelings. I never believed she was given a chance at life.

The memorial service was small and private; it was attended by only me and my mom. After the funeral, days and weeks went by, and I couldn't eat or sleep.

So, again I wanted to end my life. That was the second and last time I tried to kill myself. I was prescribed Prozac after her death. I took a few extra pills and washed them down with a bottle of Black Velvet I found in my father's office. But once more, death did not claim me, so I decided that God had other plans. There must be something he wanted from me. Something out there that I needed to do, some unfinished business. So, I never thought about or tried killing myself ever again. I knew deep inside if my family learned of the suicide attempts they would have committed me, not thinking twice about it, but now having Brent I wouldn't dare try, he's everything to me.

Even after the way the relationship ended with Brent's father, Aron, I couldn't take not only my life but my baby's life too. I began thinking back to those days, so long ago. I met Aron Bernard, the first guy I went out with since the rape, and he entered into my life and my heart. Not too many days passed before we started living our once separate lives as one.

When we finally graduated from college—a day I was hopeful would come and then was scared when it did—we now had our whole life in front of us for what we wanted to do. Since the first day I met Aron, he had never pushed me into the intimacy that was a part of every relationship he had had before me.

In time his waiting ended as my resolve and emotional wall crumbled, and for the first time since we met we made love. In my eyes the moment was beautiful because of the waiting we had endured. That wait had built our relationship in ways that mere sex would have ripped apart.

Aron apparently didn't feel the same way. He got what he wanted and he left a few weeks later after I told him that I was pregnant with his child. I thought he seemed happy about the baby; the smile on his face didn't seem fraudulent.

But then he faded into the background of my life as the days we were together became fewer and fewer until the day he stopped coming to see me, and that day rolled into weeks.

I found the courage to drive over to his parents' house and discovered that he had moved to Italy to pursue his love of art. They never mentioned my pregnancy so I assumed they didn't know; it would be just like Aron not to tell them. The thought of him having a child would mean he was no longer a child himself. He wasn't the man I had thought him to be. I now understand that he didn't worry about not making love to me because when we weren't together, he had fulfilled his needs in other ways; but of course, I'm not certain of that. It's what I made myself believe to get over him.

I sat down with Aron's parents and confided in them, telling them that I had told Aron about the baby and that I hadn't heard from him since. At first, I thought his mother was thrilled that I was carrying her grandchild as her lips formed a smile. As I knew his mother and father were rich, I assured them that I wasn't there to ask for financial help. I just wanted them to know that I was pregnant. I never thought they would be so cruel. His mother told me to forget about their son and his father stood up in disgust and stormed out of the room, only returning with a check made out to me for twenty thousand dollars. I took the check and ripped it up in front of them and said good-bye. Those people would never be the grandparents to the baby I carried so I left and began the next change in my life: as a single mother raising my son, Brent.

I wasn't totally alone; my friend Lisa from high school was a big help by taking care of Brent while I took two years of night classes to get my master's degree. When I graduated, I landed a quality job at *The Chicago Tribune*. I could finally move out and get my own place.

I used the hurt and anger I felt when I found out that Aron left, as an incentive to write my first novel, but my feelings about Aron's departure were mixed because deep down I knew he wasn't ready to be a father. Not as much as I was ready to be a mother.

Something formed around my fingers and I lifted my head, gazing into Brent's eyes. He blinked at me and I straightened up to get a better look.

"Hey, Mom," he whispered, like it was an ordinary day.

"Brent, you're awake. You're finally awake!" I started to cry and laugh at the same time. I couldn't believe he was back with me.

"How are you feeling?" I asked, wiping the wetness from under my eyes.

"Tired and thirsty." His voice made a soft whistle sound. I stood and poured him a glass of water from a pitcher on a table behind me. I helped him sit up and slid the straw into his mouth. He swallowed a couple times than flicked the straw out. Setting the cup down next to me, I smoothed my hand over his face, being careful not to touch his bruises.

"Where am I?" he asked.

"You're in the hospital. You were in an accident with Aunt Shelia," I said, not taking my eyes off him.

"Is she okay? Did she get hurt?" Lifting his right arm up, he coughed and noticed the cast, then brought it back down.

"She's right next to you, but she's in a coma. We are waiting for her to wake up. The doctors are doing the best they can with her. She hit her head pretty hard and had some bleeding, but a lot of swelling."

"So, she has a concussion?"

I chuckled. "Where did you learn that?"

"Mom, I'm thirteen, remember? I'm a smart kid, you know."

"That you are, my son. That you are." I didn't want to leave his side to notify the doctor, so I pressed the button on his bed to indicate that they should come to the room.

Within seconds the door sprung open and the same redheaded nurse I saw at the desk everyday came barging in. The look on her freckled face was priceless when she saw Brent sitting up, which made me laugh out loud and a smile formed on her lips.

"Well, hello. It's about time you woke up, young man," the nurse said as she glided to the opposite side of the bed and started checking his vitals. "Everything looks good. I'll give the doctor a buzz and let her know you are alert."

"Thank you," I said and she exited the room.

"Do you remember anything from the accident?"

"Not really. One minute we were sitting in the car talking and the next I'm here in the hospital."

"Did Aunt Shelia seem stressed to you?"

"No, she was her chipper self as usual." Brent settled his head back and closed his eyes. I panicked and shook his arm and his eyes popped open.

"What's wrong, Mom?" he asked.

I breathed a sigh of relief. "I thought you were slipping back into unconsciousness, like Aunt Shelia did."

"What? No. Just tired, is all. What do you mean, she woke up?"

I could hear the anxiety in his voice and knew I should say something encouraging. "Well, she opened her eyes for a few seconds and talked, but then slipped back into a coma. The doctor said that happens sometimes, but reassured me that everything was okay, that she will come out of it soon. So, there's no need to worry. I want you to focus on getting better."

A grin surfaced and he squeezed my hand.

"Close your eyes and rest, I'll be right here when you wake up," I assured him. "We'll talk more later about what happened and maybe then it will come back to you."

8

The heat from the sun warmed my body as I stepped outside. They had taken Brent for more tests, and I needed to stretch my achy bones. The sky was vibrant so I closed my eyes and inhaled the air around me. There was a sweet smell, like roses, which took me back to the house we lived in just a couple of weeks ago. I had planted many varieties of rose bushes and lilies in my back yard. Gardening was the one activity I enjoyed doing besides writing. When I was stuck with writer's block, I would venture out into my garden and nurture my plants, but I made sure to stay away from the plant they called May Lily or Lily of the Valley.

Back when I was a kid, I picked flowers for my mother that I had found in the woods. They were small white, bell-shaped flowers with orange-red berries, and they were beautiful. On the walk home, I started feeling hot and my head was hurting. By the time I made it back to the house, I started feeling sick to my stomach and red patches started to appear on my arms.

83

My mom brought me to this hospital, and they did some gastric lavage to me that helped reduce the side effects. I guess it worked because within a few days I felt better.

After finding a bench in the commons beside the hospital, I plopped down. Daylilies were scattered throughout the garden beds with different colors of marigolds. The roses I smelled were displayed in a circle around a flagpole. An American flag at the top remained at a standstill, then moved from the breeze.

I heard someone clear their throat behind me. I turned and noticed Officer Bates approaching.

"Hello, Miss Iris. I mean Deanna. Do you have a few minutes; I would like to talk with you?" he asked.

I gestured with my hand to the empty seat beside me. "Sure, please, sit."

"Thanks."

"So, what is it that you need to talk to me about?" I took in a deep breath and folded my hands in my lap.

"First, I want to ask how your son and your sister are doing. Are they getting better?"

"It's kind of you to ask. My son just awoke about an hour ago, but my sister is still in a coma. The only change is that there is no bleeding in her brain, they were able to stop it, but she still has swelling. The doctor said that she would come around, in time."

"That is good news, Deanna."

"So, is that what you came to talk to me about?"

"Yes and no, mostly no, but I am glad that they are doing well."

His attitude was cordial, though there was something we were about to discuss that would change how I felt about talking to him.

"Okay, what's the no part? Is something wrong?" I asked.

"Around three this morning we had a 911 call come in, but by the time I arrived, it was too late." I watched as his eyes searched mine.

"What's this all about? Who called?'

"We found this at the scene." I glanced down and noticed the plastic bag he was holding with a crumpled piece of paper inside.

Taking it from him, my eyes traced the words as I read: Call Deanna Iris to finish paperwork authorized by the Cemetery Authority for grave opening and closing and reburial in separate location.

I flipped my wrist over, checking the time on my watch. It was going on noon. I had forgotten all about meeting with Hank. Brent woke up and nothing else mattered. *Has something happened to him*? I thought. I recalled that he didn't look too good when I had seen him, but he hadn't said he was ill.

"Oh, no!" I said, certain the look on my face was displaying my worry.

"Are you okay answering some questions for me?"

"What's happened to Hank?"

"Deanna, are you okay answering some questions for me?"

"Sure, I don't know how much help I'll be."

"What is your relationship to the man that wrote this note?" Officer Bates asked.

"His name is Hank Vashon. He was an old friend. Well, more like family than a friend. We knew each other when I was young and I went out to see him yesterday. We just talked about old times, catching up. I hadn't seen him in twenty-some years. We discussed exhuming remains."

"Why would you be discussing exhuming remains?"

"Do I have to tell you? It's something I'm not happy about." My hands were shaking and I felt nauseous.

"At this time I would say you need to tell me everything so I can do the proper work on this case."

"Case?" I asked.

"I hate to be the one to inform you of this, but Hank was murdered."

"Murdered?" I gasped, and wondered why someone would want him dead. Could it be because of what I asked of him, but how would they have known, no one else was present but us. Shaking my head, I cried, "No, that can't be why!" I'd said this out loud, instead of to myself.

"Why what, Deanna? Please tell me what the two of you were talking about. I need any and all information that might lead to who did this." His hand grasped mine and I felt like crying.

"Yes, I went to see him yesterday afternoon, but we were alone. I don't understand how this could be related to what we discussed."

"We checked his phone records and he made a call shortly after five yesterday evening. Was that about the time you were there?"

"I was back here at the hospital by five. I remember because I heard a clock chime in the lobby and I looked up at it. Do you know who he called?"

"The station is checking the number as we speak, and I should know something soon."

"Would you inform me of what you find? I want you to catch the person who did this to him."

"Yes, but I would still like to know what you two were talking about. Deanna, it could help—" I cut him off before he finished his sentence.

"If I told you, you would think I'm sick in the head."

"Try me." I had to trust Officer Bates; he didn't give me a reason not to. He had been so kind to me since I'd arrived. Besides, he might be able to help me, since Hank wasn't able to now.

"I went to see Hank because he was the one who buried my daughter twenty-six years ago. She died as a newborn. She was premature. Something in my life has surfaced to make me think she may still be alive. Hank was trying to make it possible for me to have her body exhumed so I could take a look inside. I know this sounds crazy, but it's the only way I can be sure if she is alive or dead. Hank said it was all coincidence that I think my son's doctor is my dead daughter." I could tell by his expression that I'd surprised him.

"Who's the doctor?"

"Dr. Sheldon."

"Dr. Kimberly Sheldon?" he questioned.

"Yes, why? Do you know her?"

"Yes, I know the family very well. Tim and I met soon after his wife died and he's been raising Kimberly by himself. Nicest guy you'll ever meet, he would do anything for you. So, I don't think she's your daughter, unless she came back from the dead."

"Inexplicable then?" I replied. I should feel relieved by what he said, but something inside me told me different. *The guy's name is Tim and not Levin, but if this is true, then I should let it rest and take care of my son who needs me more now than ever.* "Great! I'm glad this is settled and I'm not losing my mind." I feigned a smile. "Keep me informed when you find the person who did this."

"I will and thanks for your help. I'm sorry that your hopes were dashed about your daughter, but I can assure you that it was all a misunderstanding." He stood and patted my shoulder then strolled off, leaving me alone with my thoughts. I could tell there was something else on his mind, but shrugged it off. I had other worries rolling around in my head and didn't want to add to them, especially if this wasn't connected to me.

9

The next afternoon as I sat next to Brent, I reread the report that Officer Bates had given me, "Local groundskeeper is killed. Hank Vashon was found stabbed to death in his home at 7340 Destiny Lane, early yesterday morning. Destiny Lane holds the only cemetery in LaSalle County where he worked for nearly thirty years. There didn't seem to be any forced entry, so it was likely that Hank knew the person that killed him. No personal items seemed to be disturbed. The police have ruled out a robbery. Before the victim died he placed a 911 call stating that he needed help and that he was attacked. If you have any leads to what may have happened or if you know anything that could help solve this case, please call the LaSalle County sheriff's office."

"Oh, Hank," I whispered. "Who could have done this to you? You've never done any harm to anyone."

"Mom, are you all right?" Brent asked, after sipping his juice.

"What? Yeah, I'm fine. A friend of mine died yesterday, that's all." I folded the sheet of paper telling me about Hank's murder and stuffed it in my purse sitting next to the chair.

Dr. Sheldon had told me an hour ago that Brent would be able to come home in a few days, if he kept improving. By the looks of things, he seemed to be doing well.

"When do you think I can go home, Mom?"

"The doc said it would be in a few days as long as you keep getting better."

"Oh, okay. I can't wait to see what you've done to the house and my room," he said before taking another small bite of his mashed potatoes.

"I'll have to leave for a while to drive to your Aunt Shelia's place. No one's been out there since the accident and her mail is probably piling up."

"Oh, that's okay, I guess."

"What's wrong?" I asked, my heart contracting.

"Nothing's wrong, I just like you being here with me. Besides, what happens if Aunt Shelia wakes up?"

"That will be great, but I still need to go out

there. We don't know for sure that she will awaken soon. Furthermore, we don't know when or if she will come out of the coma."

"Okay, just be safe and hurry back to me."

I could feel his worry through his words, knowing that things can change in a blink of an eye. That life as we know it can disappear in the wind. I felt sad that my son had to go through this, to learn at such a young age that we don't live forever; that we must live our life now and not hold out for something that we believe is better.

That's when it hit me that I needed to see Brice. It would take me two hours to get to my old house, and then another two to get to my sister's place. I decided that I would try to call him and let him know about Brent, and ask if he could come out this way.

I reached over and kissed my son on the cheek and reassured him that I would be fine. I set the remote to the TV next to him along with a few of the comic books I'd brought from home.

"Thanks, Mom."

I squeezed his hand and turned to leave. He clenched my fingers, so I stopped.

"Mom, I love you."

I squeezed my eyes shut to stop the tears from forming before looking at him. "I love you, too," I replied, with a smile. "I love you, too." I embraced him one more time then slipped out the door.

I dabbed at my eyes with the Kleenex I had in my pocket as I rode the elevator down to the lobby and walked out to the parking lot.

Once inside my car I decided to wait until I arrived at my sister's before calling Brice. Now that we had moved back here, my sister's house was only twenty or so minutes from us. And as we were much closer than before, I hoped we could keep in touch and spend more time together.

She lived on the opposite side of Mendota on Diana Drive. I was surprised that she chose to live out here, so close to our old home. I knew she didn't like moving away, but I never asked her why she came back out here.

I had to pass the road to the cemetery to reach my sister's. As I drove past Destiny Lane a chill tingled down my spine. Just the thought of someone killing Hank made me feel uneasy, and whom could he have called last night after I left? And why? So many questions started to surface, but I had no idea what truths the answers would hold.

After turning onto Diana Drive, it hit me that I had only been to her house one other time; we had always visited at mine. It was right after she purchased the house, and there had been no furniture in it, it was just a shell. I never did ask why that was, but of course it didn't occur to me, until now.

I pulled into her drive and parked the car. Rummaging through my purse I found my phone. Opening it, I hesitated before scrolling down to find Brice's name. I had no clue what I would say to him, and if he would even come out to see me.

I tried to sort the words scattered in my head before I hit the key, but my reflexes took control.

Ring, ring, ring.

The thought popped into my head that he saw it was I who was calling and didn't want to answer the phone. Four rings, then five. *That means I will have to leave a message. I don't want to leave a message. I want to hear his—*

"Come on, Brice, pick up," I mumbled. I was just about to close my phone when I heard his voice.

"Hello," he said.

The sound of his voice squeezed at my heart. I didn't realize how much I missed him. Though it was just a few days ago that we talked, it felt like years. Brice spoke to me in English, but with a distinct French accent. His voice was broad, yet sexy and sensual. What can you expect from a Frenchman?

"Hello. Who is this?" I could hear the aggravation in his speech.

"It's me, Deanna."

"Deanna," he responded, sounding surprised that I was calling.

"Hey, Brice. How have you been?"

"I'm doing well. Thank you for asking."

He was always so polite. *Now that I think about it, I don't ever remember him in a bad mood or violent towards anyone.*

"How are things with you?" he asked.

"That's why I'm calling. There's been an accident."

"Are you okay?"

"Yes, I mean, no, it's not me, it's Brent. Sorry, I don't mean to scare you."

"Brent? What kind of accident? What's wrong?" Panic escaped from the phone.

"He's doing fine now. My sister Shelia offered to pick him up from school the day we were moving and they were in a car accident on the way back to the house. Brent just woke up, but my sister is still in a coma. She banged her head and there was hemorrhaging and swelling. The doctors hope that she will regain consciousness very soon."

"Oh, Deanna. I'm so sorry. How are you holding up? Is there anything I can do for you?"

"Yes, yes, there is. I was hoping you could come out here to see us. Brent would love to see you. He's anxious to come home in a couple of days. You could surprise him." A smile creased my cheeks thinking how thrilled Brent would be to see Brice and I discovered that I couldn't wait to see him either.

"How about you, Deanna? Will you be happy to see me too?" I heard a hint of sadness in his words.

"That was another reason I called. I miss you, Brice, and I would like for you to come stay with us.

We can talk about things, things that should've been said a long time ago." Silence filled the air and I wondered if I'd offended him. Maybe I should have waited until he got here to tell him how I feel.

"Brice, are you there?"

"I'm here. Was just thinking about the last time I saw you. When would you like me to be there?"

"You'll come!" I shouted into the receiver.

"Yes, I can come out for a few days to visit with the two of you." I didn't have to see his face to know that he was smiling; I could hear it in his voice, which made me think of the times we used to talk. Brice and I had spoken about many aspects of our lives, even about when we were children, and our parents. There was much I had left out, and I could see he knew it by his eyes. Few French citizens have made the decision to immigrate, but Brice's parents and grandparents were among those few to move to the United States from France with the hope of finding the elusive American Dream. As a child, Brice told me that he had little time for friends when he was growing up; most of his waking hours were spent with his family.

"Wednesday afternoon would be great. Brent should be released in the morning, and I would like to stay with him at the hospital. He had a hard time with me leaving to come to my sister's residence and retrieve her mail. Besides, I would feel better staying with him; it's too lonely in our new home."

"Sounds terrific. I'll see you around noon on Wednesday."

"Let me give you my address, I'll place a key hidden under a rock by the front door. Make yourself at home, there should be some food in the frig although I haven't had time to go grocery shopping."

"No problem. I can stop and pick up food for us. You just take care of your son."

"Thank you, Brice. I can't wait to see you and I won't tell Brent. It will be our surprise."

"Okay, then. See you Wednesday, Deanna." The phone went silent and I knew he had hung up. I couldn't believe how excited I felt.

I exited the car and checked the mailbox. Letters and magazines were stuffed inside. I had to pull bits and pieces out at a time. I walked up the driveway to the path leading to the front door and wondered why she never gave me a key to her place.

Setting down the bundle of mail on a bench outside her door, I scoped out the surroundings. I couldn't believe I forgot to grab her keys, though my mind had been jumbled these past couple of days and I'd found I couldn't think clearly.

Where would I hide a key? On each side of the steps were potted plants and so I slid the first one over and saw metal gleaming there and grabbed it. It was some kind of box. I flipped it over in my palm and forced it open, digging out a key.

Once I unlocked the door, I gathered all the mail and headed inside. My eyes took time to adjust to the darkness as I groped the wall for a switch. When I found one, I flicked it on. A shaft of light poured from a lamp on a table along the wall in the foyer.

I blinked several times before looking around, trying to get my eyes to focus and the spots to disappear. All the blinds around the room were closed. At first, I thought I was dreaming. I actually pinched my arm and squeezed my eyes shut and opened them again.

I gazed back in the same direction.

The family room was exactly like our home that I lived in now.

The sofa was brown corduroy, the chairs, the TV, and even the knick-knacks that my mother had, were all the same. Family pictures were scattered on the wall in the exact position our mother had them. It was like I went back in time. I was a young kid all over again.

I raced to the kitchen and saw that it was just like my mother kept it. I was almost afraid to go upstairs and take a look. What was going on with my sister? Did she think she could bring back our parents? That our mother and father would like magic reappear?

My mind was spinning in all directions, but I knew I had to go up there and see for myself. Climbing the stairs, I stopped at the top and peered down the hallway to where my room would be.

The floor creaked with each step I took.

I reached out and touched the knob, turning it. I inhaled and propelled it open, stepping inside and flipping on the switch.

10

One of the most rewarding ideas I have ever conceived of was returning to the place where I had grown up. Many times I had thought about how I would change the events that had occurred in my life. Wishing I could return to the past and live this life over again. Then, I remember my son, and the way my heart swells every time he looks at me. If I changed any of my past it would change the outcome of my son ever being brought into the world. So it might seem odd that I felt such a connection to the house I had once loved, so much so that I went out of my way to buy the property all these years later. But as the light blinked on in this room of my sister's home I was taken back to my childhood, and not just physically but emotionally.

As I looked around I began to think this was no dream, but a nightmare, my nightmare came back to haunt me. In this horrid dream I was standing in my old room. On the wall was a poster of Sylvester Stallone and Scott Biao, just like I had when I was young. A desk sat in the corner near the window and on the opposite side of the room was my old bed.

Upon the bed was a blanket that I adored and thought my mother had given to Goodwill. Feeling faint, I reached out for the doorknob, putting all my weight against the door, and it flew back, hitting something. My heart quickened and I stumbled to the bed and sat down. I looked up at the ceiling to see the same stars that I had as a kid. I couldn't believe what I was seeing. My sister had somehow kept everything after our parents died and duplicated their house. Though I had thought that everything had burned in the fire. It was crazy and psychotic.

I steadied my breathing, gazing around the room, running my fingers through my hair to push some flyaway strands out of my face. I was horrified when I finally saw the pièce de rèsistance. Behind the door was the crib I had purchased from a yard sale with my own collection of birthday money saved up over the years. This was to be the bed my daughter called her own after she came home from the hospital.

What was going on?

The days after my mother had brought me

home from the hospital I hadn't spoken. My mind and eyes stayed away from the living, I was in every emotional way as dead as my daughter. Here was that reminder of those days though I had thought my mother had disposed of it, but of course she could have and this one was only a replica.

I couldn't stop screaming on the inside. I may have felt better if I'd just let the screams out. "Why," was the singular word I could hear reverberating in my mind.

Using the bedpost, I stood, and then walking over to the crib, I touched the wooden trim. I thought back to the first night I stood imaging her in this crib and how beautiful she was, before my mother had it removed from my room.

My mother could act like a strong woman, but in truth she was only as strong as my father allowed her to be. I knew it was my father's doing, making her react as she had to my pregnancy, because he didn't have the guts to do it himself. Deep inside, I knew my father was controlling, but at the same time he was a coward. Since the day I told him I was pregnant and that look of astonishment broke across his face, all I'd wished for was that I could again call him daddy and have him cover me with hugs and kisses, promising me that he would always be there to protect me. But before I could ask for his forgiveness a look of disgust crossed his face and that was when I knew this man with all his false promises of love thought of not his family but only of himself.

Inside were a few stuffed animals I had placed in her crib before I gave birth to her. A pink fluffy blanket I hadn't seen before lay folded in the corner with a book tucked under it. Reaching in, I pulled out the book.

"Oh, my God. It can't be," I mumbled. "There's only one way to know if it's the same book I put in her casket."

I flipped the cover open.

On the first page was a written note. I read the words out loud, the same words I had put here many years ago. "To my sweet girl, I will always love you. You will be missed, but not forgotten. Love, your mother, Deanna."

I clutched the book to my chest. So many questions and thoughts rattled through my mind. What was my sister doing with her book? I had it placed in the casket. I know I did. But that has to mean she took it. But why? My sister didn't care about the baby; she denied what happened to me. And this house, what was she doing with all of our belongings from so long ago? All these things I thought had burned in the fire with our parents. Nothing made sense to me. And the one person with answers was lying in the hospital in a coma.

Leaving the room, my internal thoughts still screaming, I shut the door behind me, allowing the secrets of that room to go back into hiding. I had to scope out the rest of the house. Down the hall was another door. I turned the knob, but it didn't turn. I tried again, but it was no use, it was locked. I remembered that we always hid a key on the trim above the door. I reached my hand up and slid it across, flinging a metal object to the floor.

I looked down and picked it up. The blade of the key slid easily into the lock. I turned, hearing a click. I once read a character in a novel saying, "Only the person who holds the correct key can open the lock and gain access to the secret world beyond the door."

At the moment I held the key and the secrets were mine to discover.

Twisting the handle, I shoved the door wide open. Now that I think of it, I had rarely been in my sister's room when we were young, she always told me to keep out. Trying to think back, I wondered if she kept it locked then, too.

I peeked inside, and then thought to myself that I was being foolish. No one was here, why was I being sneaky? Or was it more a question of what I was afraid I might find? I didn't even know my own sister. All those years we lived together, she was the one hiding things from all of us. Wasn't she?

The room was dark, so I reached out to find the switch on the wall. I jumped as my phone started to ring. I ransacked my purse for it.

"Hello?" I said into the receiver.

"Hey, Mom. Was wondering when you were coming back?"

"Is something wrong? Are you okay?" I asked, panicking.

"Everything is fine, but you've been gone for a couple of hours. Thought maybe something had happened to you, is all."

I closed the door behind me. Using the key, I locked the door and placed it back on the ledge where I had found it then made my way down the stairs.

"I'm leaving Aunt Shelia's now."

"Thanks, Mom, I'll see you soon," Brent said.

I lay my purse on the kitchen counter and stuffed the book I'd found inside. Swinging my purse over my shoulder, I was ready to leave this house of secrets. I could have spent an entire day here discovering more of what was behind these walls. As I started toward the front door, I stopped at the stairs looking up at them one more time, knowing I would be back to see what surprises my sister's bedroom held.

11

Climbing into my car, I sat in silence for a moment getting my mind straight before making the drive.

On the trip back I made a quick stop at my house to make sure it was in order for when Brice arrived and left an extra key where I told him it would be then preceded to my mailbox. Gathering what letters I had, I realized that I had left Shelia's mail sitting on the table in the foyer. I berated myself for my forgetfulness, but then realized I wanted to go back anyway to see what was in that room. *I guess a couple more days wouldn't hurt if I wait.*

Standing at my mailbox sorting through the junk mail I received, I noticed an envelope with no return address, just Deanna Iris written in bold letters. I flipped it over and lifted the glued flap, taking out a letter. I scanned over the words then read them out loud.

"GET OUT OF TOWN BEFORE WHAT HAPPENED TO HANK HAPPENS TO YOU."

My hands started shaking as I reread the letter over and over. Whoever killed Hank was now after me? I didn't understand. Someone had to be watching me, but who and why? Could this all be because of my daughter? I didn't remember seeing anyone else at Hank's, not one person was at the cemetery. I took a look around, but only saw a couple of people working in their yards raking fresh cut grass and planting summer flowers. The cars parked on the road didn't seem to have anyone sitting in them.

I forced the paper into the envelope and climbed back in my car, placing the envelope in the book I'd found at Shelia's.

Driving toward the hospital, I monitored every movement around me, watching for someone or something out of the ordinary. How would I know if someone was watching me? The only place I had been was the hospital. So it must be someone there, but who could it be? I explored all the possibilities, and those with whom I had come in contact. The nurses, the doctor, Officer Bates and Hank were the only people I could remember, so it couldn't be one of them. Hank was dead, he wasn't the one doing this; besides, what about my sister's place, and how disconcerting it was with all of my parents belongings. *She will have to explain it to me when she wakes up,* I decided.

Waiting for the next elevator to arrive in the lobby, I spotted Dr. Sheldon talking to a man wearing blue scrubs. They were near the far corner of the waiting room, engaged in a conversation. With the beam of light shining through the glass windows, I couldn't tell what color his hair was, or how old he could be. Around his neck he wore a surgical mask and stood talking with his hands in the front pockets of his pants.

I wondered if it could be her father, Tim or Levin, but I wouldn't know for sure unless I checked it out.

The elevator chimed as it came to a stop, but when the doors sprung open, I walked away, racking my brain to think of what I could say to interrupt Dr. Sheldon and this man.

As I approached, I cleared my throat. "Excuse me, Dr. Sheldon. May I have a word with you?" I was hoping they couldn't see how uneasy I was standing there. She turned and smiled at me, and I smiled back.

My eyes left hers and began to take in this man in scrubs. When our gaze connected, I knew for certain it wasn't Levin. His face wasn't the same, and even if it had been twenty-six years ago, his features wouldn't have changed that much. There would have been some similarities.

"Yes, Deanna. How can I help you?" Dr. Sheldon asked.

"I'm sorry; I hope I'm not bothering you." Knowing that I better come up with something quick.

"No bother. Are you excited about taking Brent home in a couple of days?"

"What? I mean, yes. Yes, I am. I don't know who's more thrilled, me or him?" I looked back at her with disappointment that this guy wasn't whom I was hoping to see. Well, I'm not sure if I was hoping it was him. After what he did to me, I didn't know what I would do if it was, how I would react. I felt some relief, yet was saddened by my findings, especially if this woman standing in front of me was my daughter.

"Good, glad to hear it. Is everything okay? You look ill." Dr. Sheldon reached out and squeezed my shoulder.

"Oh, it's nothing. Just wanted to make sure my son was still coming home," I was quick to say.

"Nothing has changed since yesterday, and all his test results were excellent, so I don't have any other reason to keep him here with me." Her light laughter sounded like music.

"That is awesome news, but I don't think you will be getting rid of me that easy, my sister is here."

"I'm not displeased at all that you will be visiting."

I grinned. "Well, I'd better go on up to the room now, before Brent has a cow."

"Let's hope that doesn't happen," she said, with another musical chuckle.

I nodded and backed away taking one last look at the man. I heard her apologize to him, but it was the name on his smock that made my heart freeze like ice.

Once I stepped inside the elevator, taking in a deep breath, I thought his name looked familiar.

Before I could refuse the memories coming back to me, my brain registered where I had seen his name. But how could that be. He would be aged by now. Dr. Parka couldn't be the same doctor that declared my daughter dead.

12

Before the doors closed, Dr. Parka slipped in and stood off to the side of me. It was just he and I there in the elevator. I had to say something to him, but what?

"I didn't think I would see you again," I said, breaking the silence. "I'm surprised to see you working here; I thought you worked at Palos Community Hospital?"

"I'm sorry. Do I know you?" he asked.

Did I think he would remember me after all these years? "My name is Deanna Iris. I'm Jeffery and Lena's daughter. You delivered my baby twenty-six years ago." The way his brows rose and creased his forehead, I would say that he was shocked to see me.

"Oh," he said. "Jeffery's daughter. Well, I moved to this hospital quite a while ago. I love being a doctor; I wouldn't know what I would do if I didn't come to work every day."

"Yeah, I guess you're right. So how do you know Dr. Sheldon?" I asked.

"Besides that we're both doctors, she's my daughter." Did he just say daughter, but he's not Levin? I wanted to feel relieved and happy about the news I just heard, but inside my heart was breaking, again. Though none of this explained Hank being killed, my sister's house decorated like my parents' place and the note that was in my mailbox. And why didn't Officer Bates tell me this, who Tim was. Why was this all such a secret?

When Brent fell asleep that night, I decided to write down everything that had happened since my arrival in this town, starting with the accident and meeting Officer Bates. I didn't know him well, so I scribbled down what he looked like and the questions he had asked me. I made a column with each name and wrote what I recalled about them. Reliving the conversations, I jotted them down also. One of the traits I honed as a writer was that of observation. When I finished, I dug in my purse and took out the book I found at my sister's house. I never would have guessed that she was so mysterious. No, that wasn't the word for her, more like demented.

116

I ran my fingers over the script. Closing my eyes I replayed the words in my head, going back to those minutes I was allowed to hold my daughter in my arms. At that time I didn't want to let go, and if I had known how that day in my history was going to pan out, I would have refused. God had given her to me, and even though she was conceived by rape, she was still my girl.

I opened the book to the page with the letter and read over the horrible words written. Wishing it was hand scribed, so I could have Officer Bates check it out, I then realized I didn't know if I could even trust him yet. I folded the graph I made and stuck them both inside the book and pushed it back in my handbag.

I must have been having a bad dream, because Brent was batting at my arm trying to wake me, and calling out my name. I sprang up to a sitting position and opened my eyes. I searched the room, then followed his voice.

"Mom, are you okay? I think you were having a bad dream." I heard him say.

"I'm fine," I responded.

117

"What were you dreaming about?"

"I don't recall. I'm sure it wasn't that important," I answered. To be honest, I didn't recollect my dream. I had read once that when a person wakes suddenly, whatever they were dreaming about vanishes. There may only be bits and pieces that remain floating around inside their head, but I drew a blank.

I stood and stretched, heading to the bathroom. I felt exhausted and couldn't wait to crawl into my own bed. I could probably sleep for days from the lack of rest since the accident.

I returned to my son's bed and he scooted over for me to climb in. I didn't want to burden him, but it beat sleeping in that chair one more night.

I held him in my arms like I used to do when he was much younger. As I lay there soaking in the scent of hospital shampoo, I listened to his rhythmic breathing and closed my eyes.

The redheaded nurse helped Brent into a wheelchair, as I stood over my sister. Despite the many questions I wanted to ask her, I had to wait for her to come back to us. I prayed that it would be soon, so I could put all these secrets to rest and get on with my life.

"If you talk to her, she can hear you," the redheaded nurse said.

"What?" I replied.

"Even though she is comatose, she can still hear what you are saying, she just can't respond."

"Oh," I said. "I wasn't aware of that." I bent down and whispered in her ear, "Shelia, if you can hear me, I just want you to know that I found the book I put in my daughter's casket and I will not rest until I find out why you had it." I waited for a response, but got nothing, so I squeezed her hand and left the room.

Brent dozed during the ride home. Parking the car in the garage, I touched his cheek to wake him and noticed how much he had grown. I trotted around the front of the car and opened the passenger side door to help him out, but true to his stubborn nature, he pushed me away and said he could do it himself. Though I felt hurt, I nodded and stepped back.

When he opened the door to the house, Brice was standing inside smiling at him and reached out

119

with open arms. When Brent saw him, he didn't hesitate and fell into his embrace. I couldn't help but smile at them; it was so good to see them together, again. Brice was always a good father figure to Brent, and deep inside I knew that was what my son was missing. When Brent was eight he asked about his real dad and I wanted him to know the truth. Afterwards, I could feel his pain and wanted so much to take it back, to heal his broken heart, but Brice was the one who put him back together.

When our eyes locked on each other, his dark brown orbs were dreamy looking and made me feel light on my feet. Brice embraced me. I pressed up against him and felt my body go limp, like Jell-O on a hot day. He brushed the hair from my face and put a gentle kiss on my lips. A smile formed and I kissed him back, savoring the moment. Tasting the sweetness of his mouth. I could have stood there all day in his arms, but my son cleared his throat, interrupting us. We both laughed and stepped apart, gawking at one another like young school kids.

"It's so nice to see you, Brice," I said, grinning.

"You too, Deanna," he replied.

"Okay, you two, that's enough, but I am glad that you both are finally doing this," Brent said.

I searched his face to see if he was pleased with this decision to accept Brice. By the expression, I would say he was more than happy for us.

After dinner that evening, Brent excused himself to go to his room, leaving Brice alone with me. For the first time since I'd known Brent's father, I was in love. In all reality, I had always loved Brice, but was afraid to show it. We had issues to discuss first, before we went any further. Considering the last time we had a conversation, when I told him it was over, and now after that kiss, I had a lot of explaining to do. I think deep down I was more afraid of hurting him than of him breaking my heart. Looking into those eyes, I knew it was time to tell him my secrets.

13

The evenings seemed cooler than usual in the early month of June, so Brice started a fire in the family room. I pulled out a blanket from the hall closet and lay it in front of the fireplace. He snuggled up close to me as we sipped wine from our full glasses. In my head, I tried to convince myself that I should wait to tell him my past, but I had to open up to him, if I wanted this to work. Taking one more drink from my glass, I swallowed and began.

"Brice, there's something I want to tell you. I've honestly waited far too long to confide in you." I could feel his muscles tighten as he lay next to me. My mind wanted to lock up and not proceed, but my heart said it was time to be free.

"What is it, Deanna?" he whispered in my ear.

I melted, not only from his voice echoing inside me, but also from his hot sensual breath so close. "The last time we spoke I said some things I wish I could take back, but I know it's over and done with, and I hurt you terribly. I'm sorry for that."

"It's in the past, don't worry about that now."

"Yes, but you have to let me finish."

"Sorry, go ahead."

"The last time we were together before I moved, you said I needed to open up and talk to you, to trust you. Well, I feel it's time you know about me." I took another drink, and then decided to empty my glass before continuing on.

"When I was young, I met a guy who was a few years older than me. I didn't tell my parents right away, they didn't even know I had been seeing someone. One night I went to a party with my girlfriends and saw him standing by the bonfire." The images of that night flooded into my brain. I sat up and turned, searching his eyes, before resuming. "His name was Levin, but I can't remember his last name. I thought he loved me, but all he wanted was sex. He raped me and took away my youth." I could see tears welling up in his eyes, and then a drop trickled down his chin.

"Oh Deanna, I'm so sorry." I put my finger to his lips to indicate that I wasn't finished yet.

"I won't tell you how much it hurt or what I

went through after that night, but I do need to tell you that I got pregnant." I watched his eyes trace my face and I continued.

"She was born a little under six months later. She was a premature birth, but she was beautiful. For the few minutes that I knew her, I had fallen in love with that little angel I called my own. But after she was taken from my arms, I was later told she had died. I was fifteen years old when I buried her. The doctor said it was heart failure and she'd stopped breathing." I dropped my hand down from his face and gazed at the logs crackling in the fireplace. A weight seemed to lift from my shoulders, but I still felt lifeless inside.

"It's been twenty-six years since she died, but…." I swallowed hard. "But, when my sister and Brent were in the accident, I went to the hospital where they were taken. There's a doctor there, Brent and Shelia's doctor. Now, you might think I'm crazy, but you have to hear me out first. There's no other answer to what I'm about to tell you. My son's doctor looks exactly like I did when I was her age. She has my hair, and my high cheekbones." I heard him sigh and I turned back to face him. "My old friend Hank was

124

killed a couple of days ago because of me."

"What do you mean, killed because of you?"

"I went to see him and asked if he would do me a favor."

"What did you ask him?"

"I asked if he would dig up my daughter's grave so I could see if she was in the casket."

"Why do you think you killed him? You think because of your daughter, someone murdered him so you won't find out the truth, whether or not she's alive?"

"That's what I'm thinking, Brice. Things just aren't adding up. I talked to Officer Bates who phoned to tell me of my sister's accident, and he said there was no way she could be my dead daughter. That he knew her and her father well. He said that the guy's name is Tim not Levin and that he wouldn't hurt anyone."

"And what do you think?" He glided his fingers along my neck and brought my chin up so I looked at him.

"I think she's alive, but I just don't want to get my hopes up. I met a doctor a couple of days ago his name is Dr. Parka, the same doctor that delivered my baby girl. He said that Dr. Sheldon was his daughter."

"If she is his daughter, then why are their last names different?"

"I didn't think of that," I replied.

"And you said that she's Brent's doctor. Did you talk to her? Ask her anything that only you would know?" My eyes widened and I could tell he knew there was something I hadn't told him yet.

"First, I've read a certain book to Brent since he was a baby. I was reading the book to him when she came into the room. She told me that it was the same book her mother read to her when she was young. And Officer Bates told me that her mother died when she was born. I mean, nothing makes sense to me. When I questioned her about it, she said she couldn't talk about it anymore, that it hurt too much. So, I left it at that."

"Wow, you sure have been through the wringer since you've arrived. I wish you had come to me about this. You didn't have to hold in the pain Levin caused you. I will always be there for you, Deanna. I promise you that I will never hurt you. I just want to love you and spend the rest of my life with you." I inhaled the words that he spoke and leaned in to kiss him. He laughed and we fell backwards, kissing deeper.

I thought of telling him about what I found at my sister's place, but didn't want to ruin the moment. I wanted to give myself to him tonight, more now than I ever had.

He kissed my neck, and then unbuttoned my blouse, taking my breasts into his palms. I threw my head back and let him lick my nipples, making them hard.

Heat tingled through my body as he made his way down to my navel.

I reached my hand to the bulge in his pants and rubbed, feeling his hardness. He moaned and continued to caress me.

I wanted him inside me, to give him all of me.

As we were now intertwined in each other's arms, he gently slipped in me. I groaned, wanting him deeper. I reached up and whispered in his ear, "I love you." He kissed me with passion on the lips; I could feel his tongue on mine.

"Oh God, yes, yes," I said. It felt so good, and I didn't want this to end. We made love for the first time in front of the fireplace, until we both climaxed together.

Lifting me, he carried me as I lay kisses on his neck, up to my bedroom where we made love again. In that moment I knew I could spend the rest of my life with this man lying next to me, our heartbeats acting as one.

Feeling him next to me, embracing my naked body, I listened to his rapid breathing, thinking about how much I'd missed and that I never wanted this night to end.

I woke with a beam of light warming my face, and glided my hand behind me searching for Brice, but he wasn't there. I rolled over and found no trace of last night on the sheets. They were wrinkled, but Brice wasn't next to me.

I slid out of bed and crawled into my robe that was lying at the foot of the bed, and stepped to the bathroom. Passing the mirror, I caught a glimpse of my tangled hair. I ran my fingers through it before heading downstairs.

I could hear Brent in the kitchen when I reached the steps. A smile formed on my lips at the recognition that he was now home with me. Then, I heard another voice and raced down the stairs. I don't know if I thought I was dreaming about last night, or I just wanted to be sure that Brice was here with us.

I reached the doorway and peeked inside.

Brice was standing at the stove cooking bacon, while Brent tried to butter the toast with one usable hand.

"Good morning, you two," I said in my most cheery voice. They both stopped and looked at me.

"Good morning, beautiful," Brice said, with a smile.

"Good morning, Mom," Brent added.

Brice took me in his arms. "I was going to bring you breakfast in bed."

I seized him and pressed my lips to his. The fire lit inside me last night was rekindling.

"You guys can always go to the room to do that." Brent chuckled and dropped more bread in the toaster. We both laughed and moved apart. I hugged my son from behind as I took the cup of coffee Brice was handing me.

129

"So, did you sleep well in your new bedroom?" I asked Brent.

"Yes, I love what you did to it."

"Thank you, sweetie," I replied and padded to the table near the sliders in the kitchen. Pulling out a chair, I sat down, staring out the window at the oak tree.

14

Taking in a deep breath as Brice was setting the dinette, I couldn't shake the images from Shelia's house. I guess I never really knew her, and hoped I'd get the chance to ask her why she'd done this.

After we ate, I scraped off my plate and helped clear the table, visualizing what and how I would tell Brice about the rest of what I'd found.

I lay the dishtowel on the counter, and signaled to Brice that I wanted to talk to him upstairs.

Picking out clothes and placing them on the bed, I waited for him to enter the room and glanced down at my shaking hands.

The door opened and Brice appeared with a puzzled look on his face.

"What's wrong, Deanna?" he asked.

I patted my hand on the bed, indicating that I wanted him to sit. "Do you remember the events I told you about last night?"

"Yes. Is everything okay?" I could see that he was concerned and probably thought that I had a change of heart.

131

"I didn't tell you everything I needed to say." He slid his hand over mine.

"You don't have second thoughts about us, do you?" I could feel his hand beginning to perspire.

"No!" I replied and touched the side of his face. "I don't regret anything we shared last night. I meant what I said, Brice, I do love you. I always have, but was afraid of what love can do to people." He exhaled and his lips parted with a smile. "I just didn't get a chance to tell you what else I discovered," I continued.

"A few days ago, I went to my sister's residence to retrieve her mail and take a look inside her house, just to make sure everything was okay." An image flashed in my mind as if I were back in that place and seeing my parents' things. "Her home isn't really her home."

"What do you mean?" he asked.

"The house I thought was hers was laid out in the same way my parents had theirs. The furniture, pictures, everything that they owned was in that house. Brice, they died ten years ago, the only explanation I have is that Shelia duplicated it all, but that wasn't the only freaky thing she did. When I went upstairs to check out the rooms, I went into the last bedroom, the one I slept in growing up. Everything was the same, even the crib I had for my daughter. You recall what I asked Hank to do?" he nodded. I stood and went over to my dresser, opening the top drawer, pulling out the book I'd found.

"This was in the crib, Brice." Handing it to him, I sat back down. "Go ahead, take a look at the inside page." I watched his eyes browsing over the words, and could tell he was as confused as I was when I discovered it. He glanced up at me and shook his head.

"But how did she get this?"

"I've asked myself that a thousand times already. And there's more. I didn't get a chance to look in what would've been her old room. The door was locked, and after I found a key and unlocked it, my phone rang, and I didn't have time to go inside.

"What are you going to do, Deanna?"

"The only conclusion I can think of is to go back there and search until I find something that can justify what I have already come across."

"Are you sure you want to go back there? You have been through so much these past weeks. I

133

couldn't live with myself if something happened to you."

That's one of the things I loved about him, he was so compassionate. "I don't want to live without you either, Brice, but I need to find out the truth. The only other person that can answer these questions is in the hospital and no one knows when she will wake up."

"I just can't let you go there, at least not without me."

"You want to go with me?" I asked, surprised.

He seized my hand in his, saying, "I wouldn't have it any other way, my love," kissing me with tenderness. We embraced each other and collapsed on the bed, making up for lost time.

15

"Are you sure you don't want to come with us?"

"I'm sure, Mom. You and Brice go. I'll be fine. Besides, I don't want to go back to that hospital," Brent replied.

"Okay, but please stay near the phone because I will be calling you just to check in."

"Mom, please. I'm not a baby."

"You will always be my baby, Brent, and there's nothing you can ever do to change that," I said with a smile.

"I'm just going to be up in my room playing X-Box, no need to worry about me."

That is something I will always do, I thought and hugged him one last time then slipped out the door.

Brice requested that he drive, and I didn't give him a fight.

He held my hand as we ventured into the lobby and took the next elevator to my sister's floor.

Standing next to her bed, I noticed that nothing

was different from the day before. Brice carried two chairs to the side of the bed frame. Just as we sat down the door to the room swung open. I turned to see Dr. Sheldon coming in with a clipboard in hand and a smile brightened her face.

"Hello, Deanna. Back so soon?" she asked.

"Yes, I had to come see my sister, was hoping she was awake by now, but I can see she hasn't changed," I replied, taking hold of Brice's hand.

"I see we have a new face here with you," Dr. Sheldon said, coming to the other side of the room.

"Yes, this is my boyfriend Brice," I replied and watched a smile play over his lips. He glanced over at me then turned his head up at the doctor.

"Hi, it's nice to meet you, I've heard so much about you," he said.

I searched his face when he looked at Dr. Sheldon, to see if he noted what I had. My heart sunk inside my chest because he showed no sign of believing me.

I could feel the air around me getting close. No one was talking; it was too silent in the room, like a morgue.

"So, has there been any change at all with my sister?" I asked.

"I wish I could give you good news but nothing's changed. The swelling has gone down, and there's no sign of hemorrhaging since I spoke to you last. Now, it's just a waiting game. I would like to say she could wake up soon, like today or tomorrow, but then I would be giving you false hope." She closed the chart in her hand.

"I understand, thank you for your honesty. Would it be all right if I called here instead of coming in everyday to check on her? Brent's home and I would like to spend time with him."

"Sure, that's no problem. In fact, I was surprised to see you here today."

"Brice just showed up last night, and he hadn't seen Shelia in a long time. Besides, I didn't want her to wake up with no one here, but I know she is in good hands."

"I will have the nurses call you as soon as she regains consciousness."

"Thank you, I appreciate your doing that for me." I watched as she scratched her head and a few strands of hair fell onto the blanket. I don't know how long I stared at it before Brice waved his hand in front of my face.

"Are you all right, Deanna?" he asked.

Nodding my head, I answered, "Yes, I'm fine, why do you ask?" Looking confused, I glanced at the both of them.

"You seemed to be in a trance, that's all," Brice replied.

I gave him a forced smile. "Nope, I'm good." I had to wait until she left before I could tell him what I was thinking.

"I must go for now. I have other patients to check on. I'll stop at the desk and let the nurses know to contact you if there's any change."

I watched as she strolled to the door, closing it behind her.

"Okay, Deanna, what's going on?" Brice asked as he looked into my eyes.

I didn't answer him right away, instead I reached over my sister and pinched the hair that I had seen fall, between my fingers. "Brice, I know this will sound weird, but I need to have this checked. I want DNA run on this hair."

138

"And how am I supposed to do that?" He stared at the thin strands of hair then back up at me.

"You said you work in a lab with animals. It wouldn't be any different checking this fiber than an animal's, right?"

"True, but are you sure you want me to do this? What if she's not yours?" He viewed my face, and then replied, yes, he would have it checked.

I wrapped my arms around his neck, "Thank you so much, Brice. You don't know how much this means to me." With my chin resting on his shoulder, I almost forgot to ask him what his impression was of her. "Do you think she resembled me at all?" I asked and pulled back to observe him as he answered.

"I have known you for a long time, so I have to say, there are some parts of her that look like you, but I'm not stating that you two look identical. I know you want me to say that she resembles you in every way, but I just can't be certain of that, and give you false hope."

"Oh," I said and then frowned. "You're just being honest, I suppose."

"Deanna, don't take it the wrong way. She does and she doesn't. Not every child looks identical to their parents."

"You're right. I'm just overreacting." Brice's logic made me consider Shelia and how she looked nothing like our parents or me. I placed the hair I found between two sheets of the paper I carried for writing when inspiration struck, and put it in my purse then squeezed my sister's hand.

On the way back to my house we stopped and purchased groceries at the local grocery store. My mind kept wandering back to the mystery of my sister's place. I needed to go back there and check the rest of the house. I needed to know what was in that room; maybe it would answer all my questions. But Brice was right, we should go together, but we never seemed to have the time.

We pulled into the driveway and my cell phone rang. Brice exited the car to retrieve the groceries while I took the call. The number didn't look familiar, but I answered it anyway.

"Hello, this is Deanna."

"Hi, Deanna, it's Officer Bates. I just called to

let you know there will be a memorial service for Hank Vashon tomorrow at eleven. It's being held at Falcon Memorial on Belmont Street."

"Oh, okay. Thank you for contacting me, you didn't have to go out of your way to call me."

"I remembered you saying that he was a dear friend, and I wasn't sure if you were aware of the services being held."

"No, I didn't. Brent came home yesterday and I have been spending time with him. And a close friend came into town to visit. So, I've been a little preoccupied lately. I'm glad you called, thank you." I closed my phone before he had a chance to respond. With all the surprises in my life and recent developments, I didn't feel like talking to him.

I reached for the handle and flung the car door open, taking a step out. I wasn't sure if I just lost my balance or what happened, but I gravitated back into the car. It was like everything around me went black, and now I was sitting in the car, again. Brice was coming around the corner from taking the groceries in, and must have seen me, as he hurried over to help.

"Are you all right?" he asked, extending his hand to support me.

"I don't know. I went to get out of the car, and the next thing I knew I was back inside."

"Here, let's get you in the house, maybe you need to lay down for a while?" He encircled me with his arms, helping me inside.

"Yeah, I think I should lay down for a bit." I peeked in on Brent before going to my room. My body was exhausted, so I made my way to the bed, and plummeted into a deep sleep.

I wasn't sure what time it was when my eyes sprung open. I could tell it was nighttime by the glow of the moon slipping in between the blinds. I situated myself on the edge of the bed feeling sluggish. I shuffled my way to the bathroom and closed the door, not wanting to wake Brice.

Braced against the counter to hold myself up, I hurried to lift the toilet seat before vomit went everywhere.

16

Wiping my mouth with a wet washcloth, I glanced in the mirror, seeing my complexion was pale. *I must have caught a flu virus from the hospital,* I reasoned.

After soaking the cloth in hot water, I set it on my face, letting it relax my facial muscles. Removing the washcloth, I filled a paper cup and swished out my mouth and then drank down some water. My stomach started to feel better after a few minutes.

Instead of climbing back into bed, I went downstairs. After making a cup of tea with honey and taking two Tylenol, I nestled into my favorite chair in the office. I switched on the Victorian lamp in front of me, opening the top drawer of my pedestal desk. I fell in love with this desk the minute I saw it at a consignment store, but I didn't have two nickels to rub together to make a dime at the time. After my first book landed an agent and was published, I was able to purchase it.

I flicked on the power to my computer. I couldn't remember the last time I sat here and worked on my book. I ended with eighty thousand words and still needed to browse over what I had written before turning it into my editor. I jotted down a note to call him sometime tomorrow, and fill him in on what had been happening here. Hoping he didn't need the novel anytime soon. With all the stress of the last few days, I wasn't ready nor did I need an argument over the amount of time I was taking to finish this novel.

The monitor came to life and I clicked my mouse on the icon for the Internet. Call me crazy, but with the technology these days, if you wanted to find things out on your own, this was the place to start. I typed in Shelia Larisa to peoplefinder.com, and hit search. Six Shelia Larisa's popped up, but there were only two that didn't have an age by the name. The others were way too old to be her and didn't live in Illinois. There was something strange going on, because starting ten years ago, she didn't exist. It was like she fell off the face of the earth.

Nothing.

No credit cards or loans in her name.

I wrote down the last known resident on a notepad and clicked on the highlighted address, which took me to another page. I entered my credit card number and hit start. That was the only drawback about these websites; they always wanted your money before giving out information. I sipped my tea waiting on the next page to appear. I would search for Officer Bates after this, and find anything I could on him.

The next page gave me many options to choose from. I scrolled down and tapped on birth certificate. The names of the guardians didn't match our family name, which meant....

This can't be right, because if this is true, then that means Shelia isn't my real sister.

I hit the back arrow and scanned more documents. There in black and white I found the word adoption. I breathed in and pressed the underlined script. My eyes moved slowly over the sentences. I wanted to soak in every word I read.

My parents adopted Shelia Larisa two years before I was born.

I sat back in my chair taking it all in, my mind flashing back in time. Though I was shocked, in all reality, it made perfect sense. There was not one thing about the two of us that we shared. Before and after we moved, my friends would say how different we were, and that we looked nothing alike. But it made me wonder if Shelia knew that she was adopted, and if she did, why she had never mentioned it to me; for that matter, my own parents didn't tell me.

I went back and printed all the information I found on Shelia.

My stomach felt queasy and my head ached. So much for the Tylenol I took a while ago.

It felt like someone was squeezing my heart like a stress ball and I wanted so much to cry, but not one tear escaped my eyes. I drank down the rest of my tea that had cooled, then placed the cup back on the desk.

I sat back, focusing on everything I'd found.

I stapled the papers together and hid them in the bottom drawer. I didn't want to take the chance that Brent would come in here and find them. He didn't need any more stress to hinder his recovery.

The grandfather clock in the family room chimed four times, which told me it was four in the

146

morning. I set my cup in the sink and headed back to bed, snuggling close to Brice. He wrapped his arm around me and I sighed with contentment. I reflected on all the times we'd spent together, and marveled why it took me this long to realize how much I really did love him and wanted to be with him. It must have had a lot to do with Hank, seeing him in that place, all alone. No one to wake up with or care for, it made my heart sting. Maybe that's what I needed: to open up to Brice, and let myself be loved. He didn't even flinch when hearing that I was raped; he cared, but it didn't change the way he felt about me. I think it just made me understand that I needed to move on with my life and forgive myself. Besides, I had spent enough time sheltered from the world. Throwing myself into my work and caring for Brent was enough back then, but now it was wonderful to have my best friend along for the journey.

I felt his chest rise and settle against my back and I closed my eyes.

17

I was feeling better as I dug in my closet for something to wear to Hank's funeral. I knew you were supposed to wear black, but that seemed too depressing, so I elected to wear a dark blue dress that draped past my knees.

I fastened my hair into a clip and added some light make-up and a splash of perfume. Brice offered to stay home with Brent while I paid my respects to Hank's family, but I knew he didn't have any family, none that he had mentioned to me in all the years we had talked.

Before I left, I pulled Brice into my office and showed him the papers I found on the Internet last night.

"So, Shelia isn't your real sister?" I could see he was surprised by the look on his face.

"That's what it's saying," I replied. "None of this makes sense to me, Brice."

"What do you want to do?"

"I was thinking that later we could take a drive

over to the house and look around. I don't know what else to do or how else to handle this. Eventually, we will have to go there and see what she's been hiding; and besides, I need to know if my daughter is alive or not. We're talking about my first-born, my baby girl. What if she's alive and well? I won't know if I don't search Shelia's house. I nearly killed myself back then thinking she was dead and now... now I have a chance to get to know her and be the mom I was supposed to be, Brice." Tears cascaded down my face and I wiped my nose with a Kleenex. Brice comforted me with a hug and kissed me on the forehead.

"You are a wonderful mother now to Brent, even if you don't think so. I'm sorry, Deanna. I should be more understanding, but I just found out what happened to you, and I'm trying to get everything sorted in my head. We'll talk about this when you get home. Let me do some thinking and we'll figure this out together." He lifted my chin and we kissed.

"I'm sorry, too. I should've thought about what you're going through, and all the curve balls I've thrown at you these last couple of days. I just have to know, then I can put everything to rest and we can go on with our lives, together." I gave him one more peck and wiped the tears.

Fifteen minutes later, I arrived at the church I attended with my parents when I was younger. I wanted to find peace before going to the funeral. I exited the car and stood on the sidewalk. I hadn't been to Faith Fellowship since I was thirteen or right after I had turned fourteen. The sun was radiant, and there were no clouds in the sky, it was a beautiful day.

The paint on the church was starting to flake off near the top arch, and the peeling was making its way down the outer structure. The threshold had the same oak doors I entered many years ago. Red and yellow daylilies accented the walk leading to four pine bushes that met with the stairs. I took in a deep breath and started my journey inside.

Candles flickered along the outer pews, spitting off light. The place was serene; strolling down the aisle, I then selected a seat in the middle pew. I remembered every detail of this church as if it were yesterday. Stained glass art was displayed in every window throughout the chapel. An impressive cross with Jesus was positioned in front of me above the choir seats. My sister, or Shelia, I wasn't sure what to call her anymore, used to sing in the choir.

I closed my eyes thinking of everything I had come across these past couple of weeks. I was so immersed in my thoughts that I didn't hear the person sit down next to me. My eyes popped open, but I couldn't see right away. I rubbed my eyelids, trying to focus.

"Sorry, I didn't mean to startle you, ma'am," the man said.

I knew I had heard that deep tone before. I blinked several more times and turned toward his voice. It was the pastor from the church.

"Pastor Patten, how are you?" I asked.

"Deanna, Deanna Iris, is that you? It sure has been a long time since I've seen you."

"Yes, yes, it has, Pastor."

"What brings you here? I haven't seen you in twenty-some years, I believe. You are all grown up now, and I must say, you look just like your mother, so beautiful," he said.

"Thank you, Pastor. I moved back a couple of weeks ago, to the house my parents used to own," I replied.

"That's wonderful, dear. And how are your parents doing? Is your father still working for the City Council?"

I frowned at the questions he asked and regrouped before responding. "You didn't hear?" I said.

"Hear what, dear?" A confused look registered on his face. And I knew there wasn't any way around not telling him.

"They were killed in a fire ten years ago."

"Oh, my. I'm so sorry to hear that." His face showed signs of confusion. "I don't watch the news or read the paper much anymore," Pastor Patten said by way of apology.

"Thanks," I replied. I realized, sitting there with him, that I should ask him what response I should have to the recent events in my life, without telling him the details. "Can I ask you for some advice?"

"Sure you can. What's on your mind, Deanna?"

"If I learned something about my family that I didn't know, is it best to confront it, or let it rest and work its way out?

152

"I'm not sure what you're asking, but if it's very important to you, and you need to know, then I would search out the truth, so I could move on."

I thought about what he said, and smiled. "Thank you, and yes, it is imperative that I know. It's something that I have wanted for so long, and hope that it is real," I replied.

"Well, good then. I hope I was of some help to you. No sense of worrying about what you can't change."

"Yes, that is true. Could you grant me another request?"

"Sure, what is it?"

"Can you say a prayer for me that everything will work out in the end?" I asked.

He took my hand in his, and bowing his head, he started mumbling something, but I couldn't understand what he was saying. Then he got louder and I sat listening to his words.

"Dear Lord, please take this young woman under your wing and comfort her. Show her the way to find the answers she seeks. Protect her and love her, Amen."

"Thank you, Pastor. That means a lot to me."

"May God be with you, Deanna." He placed his hand on my leg and patted it, then reaching for the pew in front of him, he stood. "Don't forget to say 'hello' to your mother for me. It would sure be nice to see her again." Then he walked away.

I shook my head wondering if he had heard me telling him that they had died. I wasn't even going to bother correcting him; he was up there in age and must be starting to forget. I sat for a few more minutes drinking in the silence, then left.

I repeated the prayer in my head as I drove to Schwarz Funeral Home. Only one other car was in the parking lot when I pulled in. I'd never had a reason to come to Schwarz Funeral Home before, so I couldn't say if there were any changes. The building was white, like the color of cotton. A beautiful flower garden was planted on the far end of the building. The stone path led to the gazebo, overlooking a pond with a waterfall. Wildflowers poked up from behind rose bushes, and what looked to be an apple tree with green apples hanging from it. The garden was breathtaking, and the sound of the water was calming; I could understand why they would seek to create this serenity at a funeral home.

Turning around, I made my way to the front. The door was heavy, so I had to use both hands to open it. I stepped inside, and it banged shut behind me. I was grateful no one was around to see me jump from the sound. An open doorway stood off to my right, but glancing around I didn't see any other open doors. I took in a deep breath as I entered the room. A few chairs lined up in front of the closed casket, and classical music floated out through hidden speakers.

No one else was present.

I walked to the front and read the sign standing next to the coffin.

"Hank Matthew Vashon, may he rest in peace," it stated. I took a pamphlet, and sat down. As I was glancing through it, I heard footsteps coming up from behind me and turned in my seat.

"Deanna, I'm glad you could make it," he said.

"Officer Bates, what brings you here? Were you a friend of Hanks?" I was hoping he didn't see the expression of fear and annoyance on my face when I looked at him. I grinned to cover up what I really thought.

155

"Actually, I came to see you," he said.

"Couldn't this wait until after the funeral?"

"It could, but since it's just you and I here, what better time to talk to you than now."

I noted his outfit, and wondered if he always wore his uniform, or maybe he was just coming off his shift from the police department. Besides, what could he want to talk to me about right now that couldn't wait until after the service?

"Okay, what do you want to discuss? Have I done something wrong? Is that why you need to do this now?" I was feeling irritable, and found myself searching his face for anything that I might remember Levin having, a birthmark, moles, his eyes, but nothing popped out at me. There weren't any similar traits in his face, but I knew it had been a long time, and people's appearances change as years go by.

"Is everything all right, Deanna?"

I blinked. "Yes, sorry, everything is fine."

"Did you know that you always say that when someone asks how you are doing?"

"Then I guess I'm always fine. My life may have not been the best since I arrived, but like most

156

people, you have to be strong, and get through it."

"You're right."

"So, what did you want to talk about?"

"Oh, yeah, almost slipped my mind. Do you remember me telling you that we were searching the phone number that Hank called right before he was killed?"

My eyes opened wide. "Yes, I recall."

"We weren't able to reach the owner of that number, but we were able to get an address. I wrote down the number and the location for you, just in case you might know who it is." He handed me an envelope from his pocket, I took it, then looked back up at him.

"Thanks, I'll open it later when I get home."

"So, how's Brent doing now that he's home? I'm surprised he isn't with you."

"A friend of mine is in town for a few days, he is staying with him while I'm out." *Why didn't I say boyfriend, which is what Brice is. It's not like I'm covering up something, he is a friend and he's my lover, but I don't need to explain that to him.* Then the paperwork I printed out entered my mind, and I thought, what better time than this to ask him some questions. He's always asking me for answers, now I'll turn it on him.

"Can you explain to me why Dr. Sheldon's name is different from Dr. Parka's? I ran into him at the hospital, and he said that she was his daughter, so why do they have different last names?"

"To be honest with you, I've never asked him why that is. Maybe she took her mother's maiden name, you know, since they're both doctors."

"I didn't think of that, you may be right. Do you mind me asking you another question?"

"No, go right ahead."

"What is your first name, that's of course if you don't mind me calling you by your real name. Officer Bates is so formal." By the expression on his face, I could see that I had caught him off guard.

The music stopped and Pastor Patten stepped in front of the casket.

"Deanna, it's so nice to see you again so soon." I nodded. Why couldn't he wait a few minutes until after I learned the officer's name?

He began to speak again. "Let us please stand and close our eyes as I say a prayer for Hank Matthew Vashon."

When Pastor Patten was finished, I opened my eyes and Officer Bates was gone.

Part Two

Courage is the art of being the only one who
knows you're scared to death….

Harold Wilson

18

Since I was the only one that showed up, the memorial lasted a short ten minutes. Now Hank was off to be cremated, and his ashes would be scattered over the lake in the cemetery tomorrow.

I wiped a tear from my face and pushed open the door to the outside. Shielding my eyes from the sun, I glanced around, but didn't see anyone. No joggers, or people walking, it was deserted. I anticipated seeing Officer Bates and finishing our conversation. I couldn't believe he would walk out like that and not say a word. It all seemed strange to me, and I had a feeling that he was hiding something. What the man didn't understand was that I would do what I had to do to find the answers I was searching for, and I would find the truth even if it killed me.

Before going home, I decided to take a quick drive past Shelia's house, and see if anyone was around, ask some questions.

Creeping down the street, I realized for the first

time how similar all the houses looked; but of course, I hadn't been myself lately, and when I came here that day, my head was set to one thing, to get the mail and return to my son.

Every other home was a ranch style, with the same colors, same details, and a white picket fence in the front yard. The others, like Shelia's, were an American Craftsman design. I almost thought maybe I had gone inside the wrong home, but even if I did it wouldn't explain all of my parents' furniture. Shelia had a lot of explaining to do when she woke up.

I spotted a beige Camry sitting in the driveway that wasn't there before. The garage door was half open and I could see another car inside, but couldn't tell the make or color, though I thought it might be red, but wasn't sure. Turning my head to the right, I didn't spot any neighbors across the street. It seemed that no one was home, or at least, they were not outside.

Just as I was passing the house, from the corner of my eye, I saw a woman with dark hair coming out the front door. I didn't want to stop in the middle of the road and cause a scene. So, I turned around a couple of driveways down and coasted back through. She was putting a paper bag full to the hilt in the trunk of the car. I watched her turn as she closed the lid of the trunk, and caught a side glimpse of her face. I was frozen; she stopped and took a quick look towards my car, and then hurried back inside, closing the door behind her.

A part of me thought she looked exactly like my mother, but that couldn't be—she was dead!

19

Maybe it was just my mind running wild hoping that my mom was here, and alive, because she would know what to do. She would be happy for me now that I had let someone into my life that loved me and wanted to take care of me.

A few months before she was killed, she embraced me, and said how proud she was of me and that she was sorry she never told me that, but hoped I knew. I told her I didn't know and that it felt good to hear it from her, but I was certain that there was something else she wasn't telling me.

I sat in my car watching the house, but didn't notice anything strange. I wanted to park the car and run up to the house and pound on it until the woman answered, but I couldn't make myself do that. Taking my foot off the brake, I inched down the road. Before I turned my head to drive away, I saw a curtain move from the room that I wasn't able to go into that day and I stopped the car. Whoever it was, knew I was here.

I was shaken when my cell phone started to ring, and I reached down and saw that it was Brice calling me.

"Hello," I answered.

"Hey, Deanna, was just wondering if everything was okay, and if you were on your way home? I hope I'm not bothering you?" he asked.

"Of course not, I'm on my way now."

"Okay, good. So, I'll see you soon then?"

"Yes, I'll see you soon," I replied, hoping he didn't hear the strain in my voice.

"I love you," he said. The connection was quiet, and I knew I should respond.

"I love you, too, Brice. See you in a few." I closed my phone and observed the surroundings once more before driving off, and whoever was hiding had disappeared from the window.

The entire trip home I spent talking to myself, trying to put all the pieces together, but if anything, I was more confused now than I was before. I needed answers, and my mind thought of Shelia lying in that hospital bed. If only she would wake up, then I could

165

learn what was going on. My phone rang just as I was pulling into my driveway. I put the shifter in park and opened my cell phone.

"Hello."

"Hello, is this Deanna Iris, Shelia's sister?" the woman asked.

"Yes, this is she. How may I help you?" I turned the car off and sat back.

"This is Kathy, the nurse watching over your sister. I wanted to let you know that we moved your sister to a regular room. There was no reason to keep her in ICU any longer."

"Did she wake up?" I asked, my heart beating in quick contractions.

"No, sorry, she's still in a coma, but all of the swelling has gone down. Now we just wait and see what happens. I wanted to inform you, so when you come to the hospital to visit her, you don't worry that she isn't there."

The lady sounded calm, and I wondered if it was the redheaded nurse I saw every day when I stayed there. "Well, thank you for calling and letting me know. If anything does change please do give me a call."

"I will. You take care now," she said before the line went dead. I reached for my purse and opened the car door as Brice bolted out the front entrance. He waved at me, and I quickened my pace up the walk to his arms. I loved being in his arms. They made me feel so secure. I looked up at him and he kissed me on the lips. My legs felt like they wanted to buckle out from under me, but his embrace kept me afloat. A breeze tousled my hair, causing a few strands to escape from the hair clip I was wearing. The loose hair teased the side of my face, tickling my cheek, but all I could think about was being in his arms. I went from being hot to cold in a matter of seconds from the chill in the air. Hard to believe it was June, but felt like March. I would tell him later that night what I had seen. I didn't want to ruin the moment.

Brice wrapped his arm around me, and we headed inside. He said that Brent hadn't come out of his room since I left this morning, so I walked upstairs and checked on him. It worried me that he had been staying in his room since he came home. I entered and saw him playing on his Xbox and went to the middle of the room, squatting down beside him.

"Hey sweetie, are you going to live in your room forever?" I asked. "I miss spending time with you. Besides, it's not like you to—"

"I'm fine, Mom, really I am!" he protested.

"I didn't ask if you were fine, but you can't just hide out in your room and forget the world exists outside. Come downstairs and have lunch with Brice and me. Maybe we can go watch a movie this afternoon, like we used to do?"

"Sure, that sounds good." I watched him continue to play his game, like I didn't exist. My knees cracked as I stood back up, just another sign that I was getting older.

"Brice and I will check out what movies are playing, and let you know, but I am not going to allow you to sit up here and vegetate. You haven't even seen the town we live in yet. I know a lot has happened since we moved here, but honey, I want you to know that it's not your fault. You can't stop living because of the accident. You're alive, and that's what matters. I will never, ever let anything hurt you again," I affirmed.

"Really, Mom! Do you think you can stop bad

things from happening again to me? They will happen whether you have a say in it or not. It's life, and it's about time you got one. I'm happy that Brice and you are together. I've wanted it for so long, it just sucks that it took me to get hurt for you to realize how you felt about him. I've been sitting back watching you condemn yourself, preventing yourself from having a life. You have no right telling me how to live when you were living that way all along."

He didn't even look at me when he spoke, and to be honest, I almost fell over from what he said. All of what Brent spoke was so true, and to hear it from my thirteen-year-old son was what shocked me the most. He was smarter than I gave him credit for, but that didn't give him the right to talk to me that way, even though he was right. My heart ached at hearing the truth that this whole time I thought I was protecting myself, but in reality I was hurting my son by not having a life outside our home and my work.

I collected myself and kissed him on the temple. "I'm sorry you think that it was your getting hurt that made me understand what I needed in my life, but it wasn't you. A lot has happened since we moved here, and—"

"See, you always do that."

"Do what?"

"You always try to change it around and make it seem perfect."

"No, I don't!" I said, a little too loud.

"Yes, you do, Mom. I'm not some character in your book, I'm your son and I have feelings too," he said in a steady voice.

My mouth dropped open. I couldn't believe what he was saying to me. It was like he was someone else, and not my son. He had never talked to me in this way before, but was it new, or could I have been so preoccupied all these years that I had not seen it? That maybe it had been building up inside him all this time?

I stepped in front of him and the TV, grabbing the control from his hands. I squatted to his level and gazed into his eyes. If we were going to have this talk, then he was going to look at me while we did. I wanted his full attention. "I'm sorry you feel this way, but it wasn't you that made me discover what I really wanted and needed in my life, and I wish I could tell you why, but I just can't, not yet."

"Don't you think I can handle it?"

"No, Brent. It's more complicated than that. I'm not sure you would understand what happened. I'm a little confused myself." I watched as a tear trickled down his face and I wiped it away with my fingers and pulled him in, hugging him tight. I rocked him, just like I did when he was a child, as we held each other. I whispered in his ear, "I love you with all my heart, always have and always will."

"I love you, too, Mom. I'm sorry for what I said, I just…I don't know. So much has happened and I don't know how to handle it."

"I don't expect you to know how, you are too young to go through all of this. But I am here for you, you just need to let me in, and I promise you that I will sit down and talk to you about everything, once I figure it all out." I cupped his face in my hand, and gave him a peck on the forehead.

"Okay, sounds good to me, and just so you know, I will hold you to that," he said.

"You do that," I responded. "Now come downstairs and have something to eat with Brice and me, then we'll go see what's playing at the theaters."

I entered the kitchen and Brice looked at me

with a concerned look on his face, and mouthed the words, "What was that all about?" I shook my head and waved my hand to indicate that it was nothing, and that I would tell him later.

"So, what would you like on your sandwich, Brent? I made some fried bananas, would you like one?"

"Heck, yeah, I would. You know that's my favorite."

"I know, just wanted to hear you say it," Brice laughed as I set the table with plates and silverware.

That night after the movie Brice and I climbed into bed and snuggled in each other's arms. I told him how the memorial went for Hank and about Officer Bates showing up. I also mentioned that I asked Officer Bates what his name was, but that the pastor interrupted before he could tell me, and that when I opened my eyes after the prayer, he was gone. I explained the drive over to my sister's house and what I had seen. When he responded, I could hear the hurt in his voice.

"I thought we were going together?" he asked.

172

"We are, but I just thought since I was out, that I would drive by and scope out the neighborhood. It's not like I went knocking on the door, asking questions." I wished I could observe his face, but it was dark in the room. From the reaction he gave, I surmised he wasn't too happy with me for going without him, but I couldn't understand why.

"What if something would have happened to you? And I didn't know where you were? I wouldn't have known where to look or how to help."

"Is that what this is all about?" I rolled over and waited until my eyes came into focus with his face before continuing. "Brice, I'm a big girl and I can take care of myself. I know you're worried about me, and I am grateful that you care so much, but please don't think you can control what I do." I didn't want him mad at me, but he couldn't come into this relationship thinking he could control me. I had been on my own right out of high school and raised my son. I searched his face and could see that I had hurt his pride.

"I know you can handle yourself, and you're right, I do care. I care for you more than you know, Deanna. Forgive me if I love you that much."

"Okay, I forgive you," I said, and we both started laughing.

He pulled me in close to him and kissed my neck, sending electro lights through my body. One hand cupped my breast and the other massaged me. He disappeared under the blanket, and I moaned with pleasure. I wanted all of him then and there.

I took the pillow under my head and squeezed it tight. I didn't want him to stop. I moaned again, and told him how good it felt. I arched my back as he continued, until I climaxed.

He kissed my inner thigh, making his way to my navel. Penetrating me, I could feel his hardness inside me, and I came alive once more. The more he moaned, the more turned on I became. I pushed down on his buttocks making him go deeper inside me, and wrapped my legs around him. He licked my nipples and slipped his arm under my back, arching me in the air as we climaxed together.

He settled down beside me with his hand on his chest, we were both breathing heavy. I would say that his chest was beating just as fast and hard as mine was. I rolled to my side and pressed myself against him, and we spooned like perfect silverware.

Brice's arm was lying over my mid-section when I was jolted awake. I took in a breath and held it, listening to the sounds around me. I could've sworn I heard a noise coming from downstairs.

20

I slid out of bed and slipped into my robe. Glancing over my shoulder, I saw his silhouette and was relieved that I didn't wake him. I crept out of the room and stood in the hall, my eyes searching the darkness around me. I stood there for a while, listening, to see if I could hear something, anything, before progressing downstairs. I looked down the hallway towards Brent's room, and saw that the door was closed and no light on. It was just my imagination getting the best of me. I held the banister and coasted down the steps trying not to make the stairs creak. Reaching the bottom my eyes scanned the room, registering nothing out of the ordinary.

Then I heard the slider in the kitchen whoosh shut, or was it opening? I wasn't sure. I gripped the railing, but couldn't bring myself to move. There was someone in the kitchen and I was standing there doing nothing. Fear knotted at my stomach and my heart thumped hard in my chest. I wanted to run back up the stairs and wake Brice, but my feet were heavy as bricks and my legs were numb. I thought if I moved too quick, they would buckle, and I would fall. So, I just stood there waiting for whoever it was to approach me.

The clock ticked by as I looked out into the room in front of me.

Tick, tick, tick, tick…

I lifted my right foot and placed it on the floor in front of me, then my left. I inched my way to the wall in the living room and flicked on the switch. My eyes searched the room I was standing in and then towards the kitchen. Reaching my hand around the corner, I turned on the light. The room lit up like the fourth of July. Holding onto the framed doorway, I took a small step inside, my eyes tracing every inch of the room. When I could see that there was no one in the kitchen, I ran to the slider, finding it unlocked. I turned the lever, locking it in place and then flipped on the outside patio light. When I set my focus on the wood deck, I could see shoe prints coming from the stairs to the slider. Reaching for the phone on the wall, I stared at the numbers and realized I didn't know Officer Bates' phone number offhand and set it back in its cradle. I remembered that he had called my cell phone, but it was upstairs next to the bed. I decided I would just give him a call in the morning and tell him what happened here.

My throat parched, I took a glass from the strainer and filled it with water from the tap. I turned and leaned against the counter, my gaze taking in everything around me. I choked on my water as my eyes settled on the envelope sticking out of my purse. I had forgotten about the letter Officer Bates had given me at Hank's memorial yesterday. I set my cup down on the table, removing the letter from my bag. It was sealed, so I ripped the corner and forced my finger along the folded edge.

There was one single paper inside, so I pulled it out, hesitating before reading it. I couldn't believe that I was afraid of finding out whom Hank had contacted that night. I stood there willing myself to just open it and find out the truth. I took in a deep breath and unfolded the white paper. The phone number wasn't familiar to me, but the address sure was.

I had to sit and put all the pieces together, but that was the problem, I wasn't sure if I had all the information. I headed to my office, and turned on the lamp. Opening the bottom drawer, I took out all the papers on facts I found on the Internet the other night, and the paper from the hospital. The one on which I had jotted down all the names of people I had come in contact with since I arrived back in this town, starting with Officer Bates. I wrote down more of what I knew of him, and then went on to Hank. He was the one that puzzled me the most because I had confided in him all those years. All I knew was that he had called someone in the house I called Sheila's. Back to the list, that included Dr. Sheldon, who I thought was my dead daughter, and the two nurses that I had talked to while at the hospital. I also put down Shelia, and everything I knew about her when growing up together.

I'll just have to go back to the hospital tomorrow and ask around for answers. Someone has to know something about these people in this town.

I must have fallen asleep in my office because when I woke my head was lying on my desk. I sat back in my chair, drool was running down my chin, and I wiped it away. The sound of the grandfather clock in the family room chimed, which told me it was six in the morning. I yawned and rubbed the sand from the corners of my eyes. I observed the papers scattered on my desk, but there was one that caught my eye. I pinched the sheet between my fingers, and studied it. I didn't remember printing it out, but I must have. It looked like a newspaper clipping, but with a photograph on it that I didn't recall seeing before. I read the caption under the photograph, "Local doctor takes in an infant baby." I took a magnifying glass from the middle drawer, and examined the picture. I inspected each person, but it wasn't until I surveyed the man in the photo that I wondered if I had found what I wanted to know. I wasn't certain it was him, because the photo was in black and white. I would have to look it up online to know for sure. I waved my mouse, and the screen lit up. Clicking on the Internet, I searched for the newspaper that printed it. I had to flip back to the date of May 20th, 1986, as my throat clammed shut, and I felt like I couldn't breathe. I closed my mouth and tried to inhale through my nose. When I regained control of myself, I did a few breathing exercises through my nose and out my mouth. I thought I could be having a panic attack. It wasn't just because I had seen something on the website, it was the date; the date after my baby had died.

After I stabilized my breathing; I glanced at the screen that read not found. "Great!" I mumbled out loud. It should have dawned on me that they weren't dealing with computers back then, why else would it not be here. Maybe I should go to the library, and see if they would have anything relating to this date? Or maybe, just maybe my mind was playing tricks on me? I looked up, saying, "God, if you're listening to me, or even watching, please tell me why this has happened to me? Everything was fine until I came back to this place, the place where it all started. I should've stayed in Homer Glen instead of moving back to Mendota; sometimes I just don't think things through." But I knew I shouldn't start blaming myself, I had to sort this all out. There was a reason for me being here and I needed to know the truth about what happened all those years ago. I couldn't sit back waiting for my sister to come out of her coma, by then I'd be so deranged, Brice and Brent would have to admit me.

21

Brice was in the shower when I came back to the room an hour later. His bag was sitting on the chair near the wall. I had forgotten that he was leaving today to go back home. I opened the bathroom door and slipped in, letting my robe hit the floor as I joined him in the shower.

I didn't think saying good-bye would be this hard, but I guess after realizing how much you love someone, good-bye will do that to you. I finished dressing and waited for Brice downstairs.

"So, you'll call me when you get home?" I asked.

"Of course I will."

"I don't want you to go, Brice. Can't you stay until Sunday?"

"Trust me; I don't want to leave you, either. I have loved spending these past couple of days with you and wish you didn't live out here, but I'll be back next week to see you and Brent. I received a call, and I've got to go back to the lab," he said.

I handed him an envelope containing the hair from the hospital, and he put it into the side pocket of his overnight bag. Then, he pulled me in close. I tried to hold back the tears forming in my eyes, but I heard him sniffle, and let them fall. He took my face in his hand and kissed my lips. The kiss seemed to be in slow motion as though my mind never wanted the moment to end. Then, as if without warning, Brice ended the kiss with a few butterfly kisses on my lips, and backed away.

Brent said his good-byes with a manly handshake, my little boy trying to be all grown up.

I didn't want our time to end, so I walked Brice to his car hoping he would take me back in his arms and change his mind, deciding that he couldn't leave.

"I should have the results back by the time I leave next Friday to come see you," he said.

I nodded and kissed him one last time before he nestled down into his seat. "I put a piece of my hair in there too," I told him.

"Okay, good thing you remembered to do that or I would've had to do another test."

"Yeah, it hit me this morning that you would

need one of mine to confirm the results."

"And no matter what we find, Deanna, I'll always be here for you and love you."

"I know you will, and I love you too, Brice," I replied before leaning in to kiss him through the open window. He backed out of the drive, and I blew him a kiss, and then waved good-bye.

We didn't even make it over to Shelia's house, but I had already devised a plan to go myself. I just needed someone to stay with Brent, though I knew deep down that he would argue with me. He'd say that he was old enough to stay home by himself, and I would give in to those puppy dog eyes like I always do.

Once inside, I gathered the paperwork I wanted to take with me, and I asked my son if he would like to come see Shelia.

In an instant, I got to hear all the reasons why he didn't want to step foot in that hospital again.

Nodding at his decision, I reached down and kissed him on his head, then closed the door behind me.

I had forgotten how beautiful this place was as I drove through town. Though a couple of the shops had closed due to the economy, a few were still left.

This street was my favorite, and always reminded me of old times. Back when people walked the streets to buy what they needed, laughing and having a good time. I had always enjoyed coming into town with my mother, going window-shopping. This was something we enjoyed doing together, just she and I. One shop where we always stopped had all kinds of angels in the store, and she would unfailingly buy me one. I still have all of them in my office, where I still look at them. Maybe next weekend Brent, Brice and I could come here and walk the street.

I turned into the parking lot at Mendota Community Hospital, and read over some of the papers I had brought. I wanted to ask the nurses a few questions in the hopes that they would know something.

Once inside, I approached the reception desk to ask what room Shelia was in. The elderly lady was kind enough to steer me in the right direction.

"Just take the elevator over there to the second floor, and make a left. You'll find the nurse's station to your right, and they can help you from there," she said.

"Thank you," I responded, and turned to leave.

Entering the second floor, I did as she said, and found the location. A nurse with auburn hair was sitting behind the desk talking on the phone. She looked up at me and raised her pointer finger, which told me to wait until she was done. I gazed around the room, but didn't see anyone else available, so I stood and waited.

"Thank you for being patient. We are short staffed today and all the other nurses are busy with the patients," she said, with a bright smile.

"No problem, I'm in no hurry anyway."

"So, how can I help you?"

"I'm Deanna Iris, and I was told that Shelia Larisa was moved to this floor a couple of days ago."

"Oh, yes, the coma patient," the nurse replied. "Let me see which room she's in." She tapped the keys on her keyboard, and I could tell something was wrong by the look of dismay on her face.

"What is it?" I asked.

"Well, it looks like she was released late last night."

"What? But she was in a coma!" I said. Unless

186

she woke up, it was impossible. But even in that circumstance, who took her, I was her only sibling. "Does it say who took her?"

"According to our records, a Mr. Ben Larisa signed her out," the nurse replied.

"How can that be, he's been dead for four years!" I shouted.

"Please calm down, Mrs. Iris. We will figure this mess out."

"It's Miss Iris. But I have to know, did my sister wake up? Did she walk out of here, or did he take her as she was?"

"Let me call the doctor in charge, he can tell you more," she told me as she picked up the phone and dialed a number.

The nurse with the auburn hair suggested I wait in the lobby down the hall, but I insisted on waiting right there until the doctor arrived. A few minutes passed, and I saw Dr. Parka stroll up to the desk, and the nurse pointed over at me. He then joined me.

"Deanna, what's wrong? What's happened?" he asked.

"You tell me, Dr. Parka. I get a call the other

day saying that they moved my sister from ICU to another room, and then I come in today, and I'm told that Shelia's husband, sorry, dead husband, signed her out. Now, how can this be possible, since I was the only one on the list to visit her, and the orders were that they contact me with any new developments?"

"Deanna, I'm so sorry this has happened. I assure you that we will straighten this all out and find out who took her," he said.

"Doctor, did my sister wake up, or was she still in a coma when he took her?"

"Didn't they tell you?"

"Tell me what?"

"That Sheila had awakened and her brain function began improving."

"And what does that mean?"

"It means several things. One, she can be put in a rehabilitation program for non-responsive patients or they can be released for at-home family care. That is, as long as there is a nurse available to care for her or the patient seeks a medical program to help her make progress. It's the spouse's decision whether or not to allow the patient to stay in the hospital, and since she

188

was improving, the hospital went ahead and granted his wish to release her."

"So, what do I do now?" I asked, feeling queasy.

"I'll call the police and file a report of kidnapping."

I nodded, and headed into the lobby to call home to Brent. I needed to make sure he was all right, and to have him lock all the doors and stay inside. Whoever took her might want my son as well, and there was no way I was going to let that happen. I started to panic when he didn't answer and decided to leave the hospital. I didn't want to cause a scene by running through the lobby, so I exited at a fast stride.

Officer Bates stopped me before I had a chance to get into my car. "Deanna, what's wrong? I got a call that someone claiming to be your sister's husband took her out of the hospital?"

"Yes, but the thing is—" Officer Bates cut me off.

"He died after they were married," he replied.

I observed his face, wondering how he could know that. But before another word came out of my mouth, he again spoke.

189

"Remember, you told me that the first time we met. When she was admitted."

"Oh," I replied. "You're right, I forgot about that. So what happens now?"

"My suggestion is for you to go home, and we will drive out to her house and see what we can find. Maybe she's there or maybe she isn't. You need to be home with your son."

"I was just heading that way when you stopped me."

"That's good, it's where you need to be right now, home with your son. I will call you as soon as we learn anything."

"Okay, thank you. Oh, and by the way. Why did you leave so fast at the memorial the other day? I asked you a question, and then you were gone?"

"Yeah, that. Well, I felt uncomfortable being there when the service started and didn't want to bother you, so I slipped out."

"I thought it was because I asked what your name was." I waited for him to answer me, but I could sense that he was trying to avoid the question again. He opened his mouth and took in a deep breath.

"Deanna, this is hard for me to tell you. I've wanted to say something ever since I saw you the first night when you came to the hospital. Since you didn't recognize me, I kept quiet, and didn't want to dredge up old memories. I knew in time you would start asking questions."

"Memories? What memories could we possibly have?" I asked, staring him down.

"First, I'm sorry," he responded, then continued. "I'm sorry about what happened to you that night."

Was he saying what I thought he was saying? That he was Levin, the same Levin that raped me? But he didn't look anything like him. Levin had blue eyes, not hazel.

"Levin Bates, but how can you be Levin?"

22

"No! My name isn't Levin, it's, Michael Bates."

I stopped him before he said anymore. "I don't understand?"

"I was just trying to tell you that I am sorry for what I heard happened to you when you were fourteen."

My mind was spinning again, everything was happening too fast. I closed my eyes hoping to wake up from this horrible dream, but I wasn't dreaming; it was all so real. I couldn't and wouldn't let myself go there right now, not until I could make sense of what he was saying.

"So, how do you know about what happened to me?" I pinched the corners of my eyes, fighting back the tears that wanted to escape. Officer Bates reached his hand out to me as if he thought he could comfort me. I moved my shoulder away from his reach.

"It's hard to explain, but I didn't mean to upset you."

"Upset me! You have no idea what I went through back then, so don't give me some lame story, like you know my feelings. I'm not sure who told you or what you know, but I suggest you keep it to yourself."

"Deanna," he said, his voice cracking. "Let's just forget this whole conversation and search for your sister."

I nodded and wiped the tears sliding down my face. "I think that's a good idea." We stood there gazing at one another until I broke the silence. "I need to ask you to do something for me."

"Sure, what do you need?"

I described the woman I saw as I drove by my sister's house, the letter in my mailbox and the shoe prints at my back door. From the look on his face I would say he was just as confused and shocked as I was. "What do you think we should do?" I asked.

"For starters, why don't you and I take a ride back to your place? That way you can check on Brent and I can take a look around and make sure the house is buttoned up tight and check out those shoe prints you found."

"Okay. And then?"

"Then, I'll go over to Shelia's and check there."

"What about me? I want to go with you," I added.

"I don't think that's a good idea right now. You stay with your son and I'll call you when I learn something."

Officer Bates followed me back to my house. I didn't recall most of the drive as I kept replaying our conversation together. I just wanted this whole mess cleared up, so I could get on with my life. Only one thought kept replaying in my mind, that I shouldn't have moved back here, and then none of this would have happened. My sister and Brent wouldn't have been in an accident and Hank would still be alive. I just needed to learn the truth behind these events. Through all the clouded ideas in my mind, one thing had the upmost priority, that whether Dr. Sheldon was my daughter or not, Brent and I were leaving this place behind us and resuming the normal life we once had.

We pulled into the drive and I dashed inside the house calling out for Brent. I gripped the railing and leaped up the stairs to Brent's room. I turned the knob and thrust the door open. It was quiet and dark in his room. I flipped on the light switch and saw him lying on the bed. Moving fast, I went over to him, calling his name.

He said nothing, so I shook his arm and he moaned.

"Brent, are you okay?" I asked.

"What? What is it, Mom?"

My heart was thumping hard and my legs were shaking as I sat down beside him, brushing the hair from his face. "You scared me; that's all. I tried calling you, but you didn't answer the phone, and I panicked." I took in a deep breath and exhaled.

"Sorry, Mom, I was tired so I climbed back into bed." His voice seemed parched and he sounded groggy.

"I'm just glad you're okay. I'll be downstairs if you need me," I waited for him to respond, but he had drifted off again.

When I arrived downstairs, Officer Bates was checking the back door.

"Do you have a broomstick? Something I can stick in the track so it won't be easy to open?" he asked. "Maybe about three to four feet long?"

I went across the kitchen to a door that led to the garage, and brought back a broom that was the length of my leg. Officer Bates unscrewed the brush end and wedged the stick down into the track and tried opening the slider.

"There, that should keep anyone from coming in again, but I wish you would have called me when it happened, maybe we could've caught the person who tried to or did break in."

"I was going to, but I didn't have your number handy and it didn't cross my mind to dial 911, though it wasn't an emergency."

"Well, if they should try again, it won't be as easy to get in like they did last night."

"Thank you. I appreciate what you're doing for me. Before I forget I need to show you something I found, it's in my office." I sat down in the chair at my desk, as Officer Bates took a seat across from me. I opened the bottom drawer and pulled out the remaining documents I had stashed there.

"Here, these are what I have discovered so far." He took the papers from me.

"What are these?"

"Just take a look," I said, watching as he shuffled through the papers.

"So tell me, what do you know about all of this?"

"What do you mean? I told you about everything at the hospital," I answered, upset that he believed I was the one holding back information from him. He had no right to accuse me of not telling him everything when it seemed most of my life was circled in lies.

"I just didn't know if there was anything else that you weren't telling me."

"Nope, that's all there is to know. Now, I just need to piece this all together and find who is doing this, and where my sister is now."

"I can help you with that. Since I'm a cop, I can get into the computers at work and run full checks on anyone."

"Are you sure you don't want me to tag along with you? I could be of some help," I appealed.

"Thanks, but I think you will be better off here with your son. I will notify you if I come across anything different." He stood and moved toward the

197

door. "Deanna, I will catch the person responsible," he said, before leaving the house.

The door squeaked open and shut with a thud. Turning in my chair, I watched through the window as he climbed into his car and drove away. I wished he'd let me go with him; I would have liked to see what was in that room upstairs.

It was useless to think I could work on my novel, but I needed to get my mind off the recent troubling events. So I started from the beginning, reading through and editing the work done when I started the book last year. A few hours passed and I decided to call it quits for the day.

Then, a thought came to me, and I searched the net looking for the site I was on when I found the article. Officer Bates had taken the paper with him, so I couldn't refer to the material I had found. When I located it, I reread the report.

At the bottom was the name of the reporter.

Ann Cummings.

23

Ann Cummings, why should that name sound familiar to me? I hit print and decided to do a search on this person, hoping that it would jog something in my memory.

I found nothing in the search. Perhaps Officer Bates may be able to learn something about this woman that I wasn't able to find. Setting aside all the papers on my desk, I went into the kitchen to prepare a snack, and then I checked on Brent.

My phone rang and I pounced on it, hoping it was Officer Bates.

"Hello."

"Hey, Deanna, it's me, Brice."

"Well, hello handsome, what are you up to?" I asked, trying to sound causal.

"Not much, just missing you like crazy and wanted to let you know that I stopped by my office and started the DNA tests on the hairs. Should know something in a couple of days or so."

"That's great!" I said.

"So, anything new happen since I left this morning?" he asked.

I had to tell him about Officer Bates, and the new information I had. But there was a part of me that was a little worried about his feelings, and that he would be upset with me.

However, what had transpired over the hours that Brice wasn't with me were not developments I had planned when I woke up this morning. I had to bring myself to the understanding that even with Brice's feelings now involved, I didn't have anything to hide from him.

"Quite a bit has surfaced after you left."

"Oh, yeah? Tell me all about it."

I brought up the papers that I found online, and what happened at the hospital with Shelia. "When I was walking to my car, Officer Bates approached me and asked about Shelia, and who could have taken her. But then…," I paused. "Then, Officer Bates told me his first name."

"He did? So, what is it?" I could hear the nervousness in his voice.

"Officer Bates' name is Michael."

"Be careful, Deanna, I don't trust him, no matter what he says his name is," Brice warned.

I knew he was right, but what other choice did I have at this point. Hank was dead and I didn't know anyone else in town.

"So, what did he have to say about what you found online? You did question him, didn't you?"

"I did, and he knew nothing."

"And you believe him?" His voice rose with the question.

"I didn't say that, but he did promise to help me find the person behind all of these events. In fact, he is over at Shelia's house right now. I wanted to go with him, but he didn't think that was a great idea, that it would be best if I stayed with Brent, and he promised to call if he found anything. I thought he was calling with some news, but I'm sure he'll call later."

"You sound disappointed that it was me calling."

"No! Not at all, Brice. I'm glad you called me. I would rather talk to you. I miss you and wish you were here. I hated having to watch you leave this morning; besides, I'm counting down the days until I see you again."

"I am leaving first thing after work next Friday," he said.

"Great! I'll make something for dinner, and maybe rent some movies for us all to watch."

"Sounds good. I hate to cut this short, but I have to run some errands. I'll call you later and tuck you into bed."

"I would love that, though I'd rather have you with me."

"I know, I don't like you living so far, but maybe that will change one day."

"Maybe?" I said with a laugh, knowing I'd had the same thought earlier.

"I love you and we'll talk later," he replied.

"Love you too." I hung up the phone as Brent came walking in and sat down on the stool at the counter.

"So, what have you been doing?"

"Just sleeping and watching a little TV," he replied.

"That sounds like fun. Hey, why don't we get out of the house for a while, and maybe do some shopping together?" I suggested.

"That sounds cool. Can we check out Game Stop and see if they have any new games?"

"Sure, we can do that, but I don't want you to spend all of your summer in your room. Let me take you around town and show you were your school is, and maybe we'll meet some people."

"Yeah, I guess. But I can always wait until school starts, to meet kids my age."

"I'm worried about you, Brent," I said, as my eyes searched his face. "You were always so outgoing, and had lots of friends. I mean, I understand we did move two hours away, but you could give some of your old friends a call, and they could come out this way for a few days. I'm sure they would love to hang out with you and see where you live now."

"I suppose I could do that later. I do miss Brian and Keith."

I noticed how sad my son was, and wondered if he was regretting the move out here. I was having second thoughts myself. I just hoped he didn't ask about Aunt Shelia. I couldn't tell him what had happened to her, at least not until I found her. What I really wanted was for this to all go away, but I did believe that things happen for a reason. Then, a thought came to mind. *What if I persuade Brent to stay with Brice for a week when he comes out next weekend. It will give me some time to myself to work all this out. That way he can hang out with his buddies in Homer Glen.* I smiled and decided to talk it over with Brice tonight on the phone and see what he thought before I said anything to Brent.

We hit all the stores in the new outlet they built over on Washington Street, and cruised over to Marchelloni Pizza shop to gorge on some Chicago pizza before heading home.

I tried to get him to talk while we ate, but my son wouldn't open up to me. Ever since the accident, I had noticed that he was distant, more remote. We used to talk for hours at a time about anything, but in all reality, I couldn't blame him for not wanting to talk about it. I knew the more I pushed, the more he would keep it to himself.

Chewing the last bite of my pizza, I glanced around the restaurant remembering all the times that I had come here with my girlfriends, mostly my best friend, Jessica Brown. She was the only one who kept in contact with me after we moved, but the last year of high school she was killed in a bus accident. She was a basketball player, and the team had a championship game in Washington, D.C. They won the game, but on the way back, it had snowed a couple of feet and the bus slid off the road, flipping over. Her parents moved away because of all the memories of her the town held. I still keep in contact with them from time to time. Jessica and another girl were the only ones that died; the others were injured with broken bones, nothing more.

On Fridays after a football game we would all cluster together, and talk about the game, or whatever came across our minds. Now that I think about it, my sister never went to any of the games, or ever hung out with me. I knew she had friends, but never saw her out with them. She liked to stay in her room, and did whatever it was that she did; yet she gave me such a hard time when we moved.

I took a sip of my Pepsi and replayed my day, and then looked at the time on my watch, wondering if the library was still open. I told Brent that I would like to make one more stop before heading home.

After paying the bill, we drove over to Main Street where the library was located. The lights were on, so I asked my son if he would like to take a look around, while I checked on something. He shook his head at me, so I left him with the keys to listen to music, while I went inside. I told him it should only be a few minutes or so, and to lock the car while I was gone. I made my way up the steep stairs, opened the door and it banged shut behind me, making an echo. As I looked around the room, there didn't seem to be many people here, if any. I went over to the information desk and stood waiting for someone to help me.

I could see an older lady crouched down on the other side of the desk, so I waited a moment for her to notice that I was standing there, and when she didn't, I cleared my throat.

I could feel my age as she grabbed the shelves in front of her and rose to her feet. "Sorry, how may I help you dis evening?" the librarian asked.

As soon as I saw her face, I knew her. She was the same woman that worked here when I used to come to the library as a kid.

"Mrs. Utkin, I'm surprised that you still work here?" I said. God, she looked so much older now. I knew it'd been over twenty years, but still it was hard to image how fast time flies.

"Excuse me, du I know you?" she asked.

"Yes, Mrs. Utkin. It's me, Deanna Iris. I used to come in when I lived in Mendota." She didn't remember me but she was nearly seventy now. She had the same accent that I recalled from so long ago; I believed it to be Russian. Her hair was as white as a ghost, with a wave to it, and it curled in just under her ears. Her hands were shaking, but just a little. I'd always loved her eyes; they were as blue as the sea.

"Deanna, Lena's girl?"

"Yes," I replied.

"It's so good to see you again."

"Likewise."

"So, what can I help you with dis evening?" She held tight to the counter until she was able to make it to her chair and sit down.

"I don't know if you can help me, but I'm looking for a newspaper clipping from nineteen eighty-six. It would be printed in the Homer Horizon?"

"Well, I don't knuw, let me zink about sat for a minute." She rested her forefinger on her chin, bowing her head. "Oh, yes. Dey just put all zese new computers in, and spent weeks scanning old documents. I can point you into de right direction, but I can't promise you dat it will be in de system."

My heart picked up speed, and I nodded before answering. "Sure, that would be great," I replied.

"See over zere, where de cubicles are?" I nodded. "Choose any of dose computers and search under de city, state, and year. You might get lucky. If not, I can tell you where we keep all de original newspapers, from up too fifty or so years ago. It has de ten local counties in it."

My mouth dropped open when I heard that they kept all the actual newspapers, and asked to see them first. She told me to head down Aisle C, and that they should be located inside the filing cabinet on the back wall.

"Tell your mozer I say hello, and zat she should stop in, it's been too long."

I wasn't sure how to respond to that, so I just smiled. Once I reached the cabinets, I saw that they were labeled, starting with the years. Finding the year I needed, I opened the drawer. Each newspaper was filed in a vanilla folder with the date and county written on the tab. I fingered through them and found what I wanted. I took a seat at the table behind me and thumbed through the pages. I wasn't sure why I was hoping it was in color, when they were all printed in black and white. But the good thing was, it had page A26 that I wasn't able to find on my computer at home. I read over the article, and then decided to make a copy of it and take it home with me. I didn't want to leave Brent in the car any longer than I already had.

I put the newspaper back in the file and headed out the way I came in. Mrs. Utkin was organizing library cards when I returned to say good-bye. But she never looked up, so I continued towards the doors and left.

Brent and I returned home a few minutes later and he said goodnight as he climbed the stairs. I wished he would hang out with me, instead of living in his room, but I also had other things on my mind, and wanted to get to the bottom of this mystery. Not once had I forgotten about the possibility of Dr. Sheldon being my daughter. But at this point with new problems surfacing, I needed to solve them first, and hoped that would give me the answers I needed.

I checked the answering machine for messages and then my cell phone.

Nothing.

Officer Bates never called me back and I was wondering if he was okay, and hoped that he hadn't run into foul play. Once in my office, I read the article. It stated that a local doctor welcomed his new baby girl, at Palos Community Hospital on May 20th, 1986, but didn't say anything else that could help me. The only other listing was the name Ann Cummings at the bottom of the newspaper. I reached for my cell phone and called Officer Bates.

"Hello."

"Hey, it's Deanna. Did you find anything at the house?"

"I didn't, but if you still want to take a look around, you can."

"Okay, when should we meet and go over there?" I asked.

"Say, tomorrow morning?"

"Sounds good, but there's another reason why I am calling you." I read the article to him on the phone and waited for him to reply.

"Wow! You found this all out today?"

"Yes, and what's strange is her name was on a newspaper clipping as a reporter ten years ago. She was the one who wrote about the fire my parents were killed in. I don't know where she works now, and if she's still a reporter, but I am hoping you can do some checking for me."

"I can do that when I get back to the station, in a few minutes."

"Great! Then I'll see you in the morning. Can you be at my house around ten?"

"No problem, see you then."

Hanging up, I collected the papers that I'd found, leaving them on the desk to give to him in the morning.

An hour later, I was lying in bed, retracing the day trying to put together the jigsaw puzzle in my head, without having all the pieces. I wasn't even sure of the shape or size of the picture I was constructing. I had thought the puzzle was rectangular, but now with the people involved I was beginning to believe it was as round as a never-ending circle. I had put together the smooth curved edges of the background, and wasn't that the basis for all great puzzle builders? You build the background with all the flat edges first, and then place all the pieces with the odd-shaped interlocking edges within the interior next.

My mind was taken off the mental picture I was building when Brice called. I filled him in on what I'd done, and asked about Brent staying with him.

"That sounds great, but if you would like, you can put him on the metro train to be here tomorrow afternoon. Then, I can bring him back with me on Friday. This way you don't have to worry about him while you figure out this mess about Dr. Sheldon and your sister."

"I have a funny feeling that she is my daughter, and that this Ann Cummings has something to do with it. But then, that means my parents and Hank knew about it. They knew that she was alive and made me think I buried her.

"Deanna, I don't think your parents would do

that. Your mother was there with you when you laid her to rest, but Hank, on the other hand, I don't know that well, so I can't say that he was or wasn't involved."

"Yeah, you're right. But I don't know. Things just aren't adding up. I could have a calculator doing the math, and still the numbers wouldn't be correct. Brice, I can imagine the full hazy picture of the puzzle I'm trying to build in my head, and I still can't put it all together. I'm at a loss here, and from the hole I'm in, I can't seem to bring myself up to the surface to see the light. But the one thing I do know, Brice, is that I need to get to the bottom of this. I can't set my mind at ease until I do." Shaking my head, I held the one paper I couldn't stop reading in my hand. "Tomorrow, I hope I will find the answers."

24

The following morning, I helped Brent pack for his trip back home, or at least the home he remembered and loved. The place my heart wished I had never left. As I told him, I watched his face light up, just as I had remembered from his childhood when he would get excited. I couldn't begin to express how much I missed those days, and the happiness as he grew up. The way he had been acting after the accident, I thought I would never see that expression of sheer joy on his face.

Brent jumped out of bed, and did this weird dance. I had two left feet when it came to the art of dancing, so I wasn't sure where he got those moves. He was smiling and laughing like he had just won the lottery, but I was happy that he was acting like himself again. After he stopped dancing, I could tell his ribs were still sore from the accident by the way he held his side.

I was able to get him a ticket for the train that was leaving at nine-fifty that morning. It was the earliest departure time I could find, not that I was in a hurry to get rid of my son. I had to say good-bye to Brice, and now I was saying good-bye to Brent. Did my entire life have to turn upside down?

I called Officer Bates and left a voicemail on his phone to let him know that I would be back at the house before ten-thirty.

I tried calling his phone on the way home, but only got his voicemail, again. Something was up; I could feel it in my bones. I replayed our conversation from last night, and was sure I heard him correctly about meeting at my place this morning. I pulled into the driveway and went inside to wait.

When I glanced at the clock, I noticed that it was going on eleven. I was certain he wasn't coming, but why wouldn't he have called me if something came up? I decided to give it a shot and called the police station. I asked if Officer Bates was in, but the officer that answered the phone said he hadn't seen him since yesterday when he came into the station to run a report. I asked if the officer knew what he was checking on, but the officer replied that he couldn't give out that information. So, I left my name and number and requested that Officer Bates call me when he got in.

After hanging up the phone, I knew there was no way that I was going to sit useless in this house. It was way too quiet for me. I was so accustomed to the noise around me, I couldn't think without it. I headed into the kitchen and filled a glass of water, then decided that I wasn't going to stay here any longer. I needed to know the truth, so I flung my purse over my shoulder and closed the front door behind me. I left a note taped to the front door, telling Bates where I went.

Thirty minutes later, I was pulling along the side of the road across from Shelia's driveway. Scoping out the house, I found nothing different, except that the beige Camry was missing. Taking in a deep breath, I decided that it was time to do this. I needed this to all be over with, and find out if my daughter and my mother were still alive.

As I walked up the path to the front door, I hesitated before climbing the steps. Reaching into my purse, I retrieved the key from the other day. Before inserting the key into the lock, I looked over my shoulder to see if anyone had followed me. I had the feeling that someone was watching me. I shook it off and turned the knob, until I heard a click and pushed the door open.

Just like before when I was here, all the blinds were closed. I flicked the switch on the wall and waited for the lamp to turn on, but nothing happened. With the door still ajar, I used the sunlight to find the stand that the lamp sat on, and clicked the dial.

Still nothing.

I checked for a bulb, and there was one, but that could mean it was burnt out. I pulled open the first drawer and scanned through it, then moved to the next one. My hand came across what felt like a flashlight. Grasping it, I pushed the button and it turned on. I positioned the light under the table and saw that the lamp was plugged in. So, it must be a burnt bulb, after all.

I shut the front door and ventured into the living room where I had seen the pictures and furniture; nothing was different. I flipped on the light and turned off the flashlight in my hand.

The room came alive.

The last time I was here, I didn't look at

everything and wanted to search it all on this visit.

I started with the photos on the wall to my left, observing each one up close. After the fourth frame, I knew that they were my mother's. Working my way around the room, I stood in front of the mantle where I saw several new pictures that I hadn't seen before. I reached out and took the wooden frame in my hand; I needed to get a better look at it.

In the picture, my mother and sister were standing near a beautiful lilac bush; but what caught my eye was the date at the bottom of the photo. It was taken almost a year ago, which meant….

My mind stopped when I heard a floorboard creak from behind me. I froze and hesitated before turning around to see who or what it was, but I didn't have to look; the person spoke to me.

25

It was like a soft whisper floating in the air. The same low sounds I'd heard so many times before, but knew it couldn't be real. This all had to be a dream, but I knew it wasn't. "You shouldn't be here, you know. He will hurt you if he knows you were here, in his house," the voice said.

I turned and saw my mother standing before me. I pinched myself as if I were dreaming, but I felt the pain running through my arm as I held the skin between my fingers.

"Mom, is it really you?" I asked.

"Yes, it is I, my darling Deanna."

"But how? I thought you were dead." My heart was racing. I moved closer to her, and we were now face to face. I couldn't believe my mother was standing before me. She was real, and alive. I waited for her to respond, but she didn't.

I cupped her face in my hands and smiled, then she wrapped her arms around me, and we hugged.

"I saw your house burn down, right in front of my eyes. None of this makes any sense to me. How are you here?" I kept asking.

She pulled me away and gazed into my eyes. "You are smart enough to figure things out on your own."

"That was only because I moved back here, and all these weird events started to surface. Shelia and Brent were in an accident, and then I met Dr. Sheldon, who I think looks exactly like me, and Hank was killed because of what I asked him to do for me." That's when I remembered that he had called here that night before he was killed. "Mom, did you talk to Hank the night he called here?"

"Yes. Yes, I did. But…." She looked away, staring down at the floor.

"But what? What did he say to you?"

"He told me that you had come to see him, and what you wanted him to do," she said with a sigh.

"How could that have gotten him killed?" I asked.

"He listens to my conversations."

"Who listens to your conversations?" I protested.

"I can't tell you that yet. It isn't time. You should go, far away."

"Time for what!" I said, a little too loud. "Why is everything a secret? And just so you know, I found out that Shelia was adopted." I watched as her eyes widened, and she took a step back.

"Deanna, you must stop. Stop looking for answers, and leave. Leave town now and never come back."

Now my head was spinning. My own mother was telling me to get out of town and never come back, but there had to be some explanation for her to say that to me. After thinking she was dead all these years, and now having found her, I was hearing that she wanted me to leave.

"I can't do that, Mother. It all started when Shelia and Brent were in the car accident and I saw Dr. Sheldon." She could know the truth, the truth that the doctor was my daughter.

"Mom, is Dr. Sheldon my daughter, the one we buried together? You need to tell me." She just stood there, not saying a word. "Please Mom, tell me the truth," I begged.

"You'd better go before he finds you're here."

"What? No, I'm not going anywhere without you! You have to come with me." As I tried to plead with my mother to leave, we both turned our heads to the sound of a car door slamming. She raced to the door and locked it, then turned off the light in the living room. I could hear boots plodding up the walk. She grabbed my arm and we fled up the stairs to the room that was locked when I came here last. She pulled me inside with her and closed the door, locking it. The room was so dark; I couldn't see my mother or myself.

Trying to be as quiet as possible, I whispered, "Mom, what are we doing?" I then asked, "Why can't you leave?"

"You wouldn't understand," she said. "I don't know what he would do if he knew you were here."

My eyes began to focus on what was around me in the room. I wasn't certain what I saw because of the lack of light coming into the room. I started to move forward, but she pulled me back to her.

"Stay," she whispered. "He will come up here. He always comes up here to see me. I need to hide you in the closet until he leaves again."

"Who is he?" I asked. "Why won't you tell me who this guy is? Do I know him?" As scared as I was, I couldn't stop the questions from flowing out of me. I had to know and maybe, just maybe, I could stop all of this. I could save her, and get her out of this house once and for all. But I didn't even know why she was being held here, and who was keeping her a prisoner. She opened the closet door and gave me a push.

"Go inside, and sit near the far back corner, I will let you out after he leaves and, I promise, we will talk then." I did as she asked, and crept inside. If I thought the other room was dark, it was even darker in here. Using the wall as a brace, I leaned up against it, using my other hand to move the clothes on the hangers away from me. Once I got to the end, I squatted down. Sitting there with my mind racing, I tried to piece together everything that had happened since I'd moved back.

I turned and pressed my ear against the wall, hoping I could hear what was going on, but it was too quiet out there. My cell phone started to vibrate, and I was relieved that I had turned the ringer off before coming into the house. I pulled the phone from my purse and saw that it was Officer Bates calling. I wasn't sure if I should answer it, just in case the man in the house could hear me talking. I thought against it. It wasn't just my life on the line, but my mother's too, and I wasn't willing to take the chance of losing her again. Besides, if I didn't answer and he went to my house, then he would know I was missing and come looking for me.

The phone stopped then started vibrating again, but this time it was a different number. A number I had seen before. My mind flashed back to the paper Officer Bates had given me at the memorial, the letter I had opened that night.

The call was coming from inside the house.

26

If I answered it, then the person would know where I was, so I voted against it, and held down the off button. I set the phone back inside my bag and realized that my heart was beating fast and hard. I was beginning to sweat from the lack of air in this small enclosed space. Lifting my hand, I placed two fingers against the side of my throat, and felt the beat pulsating fast. I began to pray, hoping that this would all be over soon. I needed to get my mother out of the house, but how was I going to do that if she didn't want to leave.

The door to the closet opened and I pressed myself against the corner waiting to be told it was clear to come out, but no words came.

"I think you should wear this today," the voice said. And I knew right then that it wasn't my mother talking. The voice was a man's voice, but not one I recognized. Looking from the corner of my eye, I saw his arm reaching in and pulling an outfit from a hanger. Wishing that I'd seen his face, then I would know who he was.

"Thank you," I heard my mother say, and the door closed. Again, I found myself plunged into complete darkness. I don't know how long I was there, but it felt like hours before light poured into the closet, and I could see again. She told me that it was safe to come out, that he was gone. Crawling to the door, I pulled myself up, looking into my mother's face. Once my eyes came into focus, I could see the room. I moved past my mother and headed to the wall, but she grabbed my arm and pulled me to her.

I could tell that she didn't like me seeing all of this, and asking questions, but I wasn't going to stop until I had the answers I needed.

"Deanna, I can't tell you who he is. All I can say is that he's not the person you knew back then. I wish I knew why he did what he did, but he won't tell me. I know you don't want to hear this, but it does have to do with your baby. That's all he told me when I was confined to this room. I'm only allowed to leave when he gives me permission."

I didn't understand what she was saying, but thought about the day my baby was pronounced dead. I replayed that day over and over, and it hit me that they wouldn't let me see her again. The nurse had taken her away. I was so young, and didn't think about deception back then. I didn't know that it was my right to see her.

I knew my mother wasn't going to tell me anymore then she already had, and thought she was doing so to keep me from harm. I scoped out the room. There were newspaper clippings and photos plastered all over the walls. My mother sat down in the chair near the window. I walked over to the photos to get a better look. There were several pictures of me at my home in Homer Glen. Shots of Brice and Brent; I was seeing my life all over again, after I had lived it. Everything I did was on these walls, except when I was inside my house.

"Mom, who took these pictures of me?"

"I did," she replied.

"But why? Why didn't you come see me? Why couldn't I know that you were alive and well?"

"It wasn't just me; he was there to make sure I didn't overstep my boundaries. I was allowed to see you, but only from a distance. I was okay with that because I could at least know that you were okay."

There were no pictures of Shelia on the wall, but I figured that was because she lived here. I turned to ask her, "Did Shelia know that you were alive?"

"Yes, she knew, and promised me she wouldn't tell anyone."

"Does she know about the adoption?"

"No!" she shouted. "She must never know. You have to promise me that you won't tell her," she pleaded.

"Why shouldn't she know? And why is it a secret?"

"I just don't want her to get hurt, and think she wasn't loved."

"Okay, I won't, but you have to tell me something."

"What is it that you want to know?"

"Is Dr. Sheldon my daughter?"

"I don't have that answer."

"You don't have it, or you won't tell me?" By the look on her face, I could see she wasn't going to tell me. "Okay, when I came here the last time, were you in this room when I unlocked it?"

"Yes, I hid in the closet when I saw you coming up the walk."

"Does Levin Bates have anything to do with this?"

"If you mean is he the one holding me here, no."

"But why shouldn't I know that you're alive? Who is this person?"

"Deanna, my dear, I can't and won't tell you who he is. It would make things worse for me."

"Worse! Don't you think things are bad now? Don't you think that this needs to stop and we can be together again? So, you're saying that this man is keeping you here, and that he killed Hank because I wanted to reopen my daughter's grave, and what then? Would I find out that she wasn't in the casket? That she is alive and well? Do you know who took her from me, and why? You need to tell me, Mom. When I was here, I found the book that I thought was put in her casket. Why did you have it, and how did you get it?"

"You need to stop asking questions, it will only get you hurt or even killed. You know too much now, and I'm not strong enough to bear the weight of losing you again. You were always the one that asked a lot of questions when you were a young girl. I can see that hasn't changed."

I could feel my blood boiling. I was getting angry with my mother for holding back on me. I just wanted her to tell me the truth, but she wouldn't budge. She just sat there staring at the wall. She wouldn't even look at me, as if I had disappointed her. "So, I'm just supposed to walk out of this house and pretend that you're not alive, and move on with my life? Is that what you want me to do?"

"Yes. I want you to leave and move back to where you came from." The words she spoke sunk in, but I didn't want to believe she meant them.

"I don't know if I can do that, Mother. I thought you were dead for ten years, but you've been alive and well, living in this house that looks exactly like the house we had when I was young." Then it hit me. "Are you saying that because of what happened when I was fourteen, that people had to get hurt or worse, die? Because if that's what you're trying to tell me then I need to find out why. What does me getting raped and having a baby have to do with you being held hostage? Did I have something to do with Hank's murder, and don't let me forget, Shelia's adoption? Mom, you can beg me all you want to keep me from

230

finding the truth, but I'm not going to stop. I'm not going to quit until I get you out of here, and I know why all this has happened!" My voice was loud now and insistent.

It pained me to watch as tears cascaded down her face as I screamed at her, but it was true, I wasn't going to stop searching for the answers. Part of me wanted to make her believe that I would stop just to set her mind at ease, but in the moment, I wasn't able to think of anything but my need for answers that all the people around me seemed to know, while I was in the dark.

I squatted down in front of her and lifted her chin. Throughout my entire life, I don't think I'd ever seen my mother cry. Once at my daughter's funeral, but there was no other time I had seen her shed a tear, and felt ashamed of myself, though I used to hear her cry in the bathroom. So, I knew then that I would have to lie to her, and make her think I would stop searching.

"I'm sorry, Mom. I'll stop. I promise. Don't cry, please." I took her in my arms and held her tight. I knew I would have to leave soon, but I didn't want to go. I didn't know whom I could trust in this town, and my thoughts went to Officer Bates. *I wonder if he is involved in all of this or if my mom was telling the truth, that he doesn't know anything.* I understood what I needed to do, and the risks I was willing to take.

27

I had to erase my emotions stemming from what I was going to do. A part of me was dying inside. I kissed her on the cheek and gazed into her eyes, and then I walked out, closing the door behind me. My heart was torn to pieces, knowing I had to leave her here, and come back for her with Officer Bates. Once in my car, I glanced up at the window and saw her watching me. I waved as a tear rolled down my face, but without hesitation, I drove away. When I was far enough from the house, I dug out my cell phone and turned it on. I listened to the voicemail that Officer Bates had left, and knew in my heart that it wasn't him doing all of this. I called him back, asking if he'd meet me at my house in fifteen minutes.

I opened the garage door and pulled inside, and as I looked up in my rearview mirror I saw him pulling in behind me. I climbed out and waved him towards me, then shut the garage door once he was inside. We stood with just the light from the garage door beaming around us. I was a little nervous, oh, why lie to myself.

I was frightened being alone with him. Preoccupied by my thoughts, I couldn't hear what he was saying, until he touched my arm, and then I jolted back to life.

"Deanna, are you okay?" he asked.

"What? Yeah, I'm fine."

"Do you want to go inside?" he asked, peering into my eyes.

"No, we can't!" I said, sounding louder than I intended. "I think we should stay out here to talk." From the expression on his face, I realized he thought I had lost my mind.

"Okay? But why?"

"I don't know if we're being watched, or if someone is listening to us, so I think it's best if we stay out here," I said in a low voice, and went to the stairs just before the light on the garage door went black, and then flicked on the light. "I need to ask you a few questions before I confide in you."

"Sure, what is it that you need to know?"

I gathered a couple of chairs from the back wall and placed them to face each other. I gave him a nervous smile, but a smile nonetheless. In all my years of therapy working through my feelings, this was where it had led. I needed closure with my past in order to move forward. Questioning my comfort level on whether I felt cozy sitting here with him or not, I also questioned my sanity. No, I did not feel comfortable, but I had to do this.

I heard him clear his throat, and I raised my head to look at him. I took in a deep breath, no, several deep breaths before I was ready to speak to him.

"I need you to tell me how you know about what happened to me. You never finished explaining it." I stood and opened the refrigerator in the corner of the room, taking out two bottles of water. I handed one to him and he thanked me for it. I twisted the cap off the other, drinking down half the bottle before sitting back down.

"It's quite a long story. Are you sure you want to talk about that and not about where you were?"

I was getting the impression that he was hiding something from me. Something he didn't want me to know, and I decided to just let it go for now and focus on getting my mother out of that house.

I swallowed and then answered, "Okay, but first I need to know that I can trust you, and that you are who you say you are. You were supposed to meet me here this morning, but you never showed, so where were you and what were you doing?"

"I was finishing up on some leads that I had about your sister."

"And what leads do you have? Do you know where she is?" I wanted to hear what he had to say before confirming my hunch.

"Well, the guy that claimed to be her husband wasn't her husband."

"So who was he?"

"That part I haven't uncovered yet, but I'm certain it wasn't him, he is dead. I had the judge sign a petition to inspect the records at Holy Cross Cemetery and did a quick check on the records that were in his medical file. They matched. So, whoever it was had a fake ID, and since no one at the hospital had ever seen him before, they wouldn't have questioned who he was, and if he was her husband. Spouses have every right to release their loved ones. That is all I have right now. So, what did you find out?"

"Since you found out about her husband, I know it isn't him keeping her a prisoner."

"Who's being kept as a prisoner?"

"My dead mother."

"Wait! Your mother is alive?"

"Alive and well. It seems this man has been holding my mother in that house since the fire."

"What? I'm a little lost, go back and start from the beginning."

I started with dropping Brent off at the train station, and then coming back here to wait for him. I went on to tell him what happened when I arrived at Shelia's house, or should I say my mother's house, and the photo I found on the mantel. I filled him in on what we chatted about before and after the man came to the house, and when I hid in the closet upstairs. I think by the look on his face, he was just as stunned as I was when I saw my mother for the first time in ten years.

"So, you're saying that this person is keeping her there? Do you know who he is?"

"I won't say I didn't think it was you because for the longest time, I did. You acted strange around me, but that's only because of something I didn't know yet. My mother kept repeating that I needed to leave this town and never come back, or he would hurt me, and possibly kill me, if I stayed."

"What?" he shouted. "What do you want to do? Because I can get the officers at the station together, and we can take her out of the house."

"You could do that, but then what about this man? What if he isn't there when you go, how will we catch him and keep him from coming after her, or me for that matter?"

"I'll have your mother put in a safe house."

"Okay, then what do I do to keep safe?"

"Is there somewhere you can go for a while, maybe out of town?"

"Yes, there is, but do you think I should? Couldn't I stay with my mother?"

"Whatever you want to do just let me know. I owe you this, Deanna. I know it doesn't change anything, but I will prove to you that I'm a good guy, and that you can trust me." His words touched my heart in a way that was hard to explain, but I guess if I would have been forced to define it, I would say that they made my heart feel warm inside.

"I did think it was you, that's why I had to question you first."

"That makes sense. I would most likely do that, too. Is there anything else you haven't mentioned?"

I filled him in on everything else, from my parents adopting Shelia to finding the book I had left in my daughter's casket. I could sense that he was trying to put all the pieces together, just as I had been doing, but judging by the expression on his face, he was just as confused as I was.

"Now, I have one question for you, Deanna."

"Okay, what is it?"

"When I went to your sister's house, why didn't I find your mother and all the items that you mentioned?"

"I don't know. I didn't think of that."

"The house I went to is on Cedar Avenue, at least that is what the computer in my car gave me."

"Cedar Avenue? Shelia lives on Diana Drive."

"What was the house number?"

I gave it to him.

"Now, I can see how you got them mixed up. Shelia's house number is around the corner from your mother's place."

239

"Oh," I said. "I guess I made a mistake, but a good one; otherwise, I would never have found my mother."

"It was a good one," he said, and then grinned. "This is what I'm going to suggest. I will talk to my Captain, get a squad car over to the house, and pull her out. I will call you when it's done, and you can stay with her until we catch the guy, but you can't say anything to anyone, not even your son. We can't take the chance of him eavesdropping on your conversation, and finding you two. That would put you in harm's way. And I'm not willing to take that chance, not when we can catch this criminal and put him away," he explained.

I nodded, even though I couldn't bear not telling Brent or Brice where I would be. I couldn't and didn't want them to worry about me.

Before leaving, Officer Bates checked for any bugs planted in my house, but was unsuccessful. I locked the front door behind him and checked all the other doors and windows that could be used to enter my home.

I called Brice before heading to bed, but instead of being honest with him, I said that I was going out of town to meet my editor about doing a book tour. It broke my heart to have to lie to him, but I didn't want to take the chance on this man listening in on our conversation. And besides, I didn't want to get Brice or Brent involved in all of this. It was bad enough that he knew what I'd told him when he was here, with the DNA test he was conducting. I wouldn't be able to live with myself if something happened to either of them. I said goodnight and decided to take a long hot bath, to relax my mind after today's events.

I put my finger into the water, checking the temperature. I wrapped my hair into a bun and undressed. Slipping into the water, I felt it embrace my weary body with its warmth. The light from the candles cast shadows on the walls around me. I closed my eyes and let the day's worries drain out of me. But all I could think about was my mother, and that she was alive. Though I still needed answers to why and who was doing all of this. I tried to fight the thought that it was all because of my baby and me.

28

The bath from the night before helped me sleep, I mused as I climbed out of bed and pulled on my robe. I came downstairs and poured myself a cup of the coffee that I'd programmed to be waiting for me. It was too quiet in the house, so I picked up my phone and called Brent.

When I talked to Brice last night, he had said that he was out with some friends, and that I should call back in morning. I didn't even think to look at the time until I reached his voicemail; it was a little after six in the morning. I left a short message to have him call me when he got up.

I took a sip from my coffee cup and sat down at my desk in the office. Moving the mouse, I waited for my computer to come alive. I hadn't checked my emails in a couple of weeks, so it didn't surprise me that I had over one hundred in my inbox. Sifting through them, I deleted the spam like store ads, and those that stated 'you have revenue money waiting for you.' Once in the past, I had clicked on the website that came with the email, and wouldn't you know, I caught a virus and had to buy a new computer because it had washed out my memory, and wouldn't let me log back on.

After I was done, I was left with fifteen emails to sort through. Starting from the bottom, I worked my way up. I scanned the bank emails and filed them in a folder for future reference. The next one was from the realtor that sold me this house, so I clicked on it and read the letter she had sent me. It was more of a "thank you" letter than anything, so I deleted it and moved on. There were a couple from my editor, but nothing that said he needed my work right away. I had forgotten all about calling him the other day and was thankful that he'd emailed me instead. He was nice enough to suggest I take my time and wrote that he would contact me in a week or so. I replied that I'd received his email and would finish the manuscript soon and send it off to him. I thought after I was done with this, I would start revising again and send it, giving him something to do. The remaining emails were from my friends back home, forwarded jokes, nothing more. I read them, and hit delete.

Sitting back in my chair, I sipped my coffee, and thought about what I was going to do with my day. Officer Bates said he would call me after he had spoken to his Captain about the situation at my mother's house. Setting my cup down, I went upstairs and put on my sweats and a comfy shirt. Whenever I wrote, I would wear something comfortable, like my sweats, so I felt more relaxed.

It didn't faze me when the clock in the family room gonged three times. I was so engrossed in my story that I hadn't heard the clock all day, until now. I reached for my phone and checked for any messages from Brent or Officer Bates. I would have heard my phone ring if they'd tried to call. I hit the recent call button, and redialed Officer Bates' number. He answered on the second ring.

"Hey, it's Deanna. Just thought I'd give you a buzz, and see what you learned this morning."

"I'm just waiting for my Captain to get back to me. He said he had to clear it with his boss, and so on. I guess I was hoping that he would agree to it, and we'd have her out by now, but so far nothing."

"Oh," I replied and then paused, before going

on. "What do you think the hold-up is?"

"I'm not sure, but I hope they come to a decision soon. I don't want to leave your mother in that house much longer. But what good would it do if we trample her rights by knocking on the front door and pointing guns, screaming for everyone in the house to get down. Whoever was keeping her could be watching as we take your mother away in an ambulance. And then, we would have other, legal issues. If this person has done all that we think he has then he knows a lot about the law, and how to work not only within it, but also around it. We haven't received any complaints from the neighbors; right now we have no real evidence, so we have nothing on our side but my word, and yours. The circumstance of meeting 'a need for immediate aid' has to be met in a legal standard for the forced entry."

"What? That doesn't make sense. Our knowledge should be more than justification to go in. Maybe you should talk to him, and find out what's taking so long?"

"Okay, I'll do that."

"Officer Bates."

"Yes."

"Can you please call me or text me and let me know what's going on?"

"Yes, Deanna, I'll let you know."

"Thanks," I said and hung up. I could feel my heart pounding through my chest, and was becoming agitated. Why didn't his boss admit that something weird was going on in that house? I was just about to head over to the police station when a text came through from Officer Bates, stating that they were going there. I replied back, "Great", and shut the front door, returning to my study. I had to keep myself busy now that I knew they were proceeding with the rescue.

By the time I'd gone halfway through the revision of my book, another text came in. It was from Brent stating he was going out again, and that he would give me a call tomorrow. I texted back saying okay, and that I missed and loved him, and to be careful. He replied ditto with a smiley face. I couldn't help but grin at that.

Time was moving fast, as I started clicking off the hours, instead of the minutes, since I'd heard anything from Officer Bates. It was driving me crazy not knowing. So, I shot him a text. "I've been waiting all day," I mumbled, into the empty room. "What could be taking so long?"

I sat at my desk typing and adding changes to my book, and by nine I was finished and sent it off to my editor. I turned off the lamp and made my way to the kitchen to make a hot cup of tea with honey. As I leaned against the counter, my eyes focused on the front door that was half opened, and wondered if I had forgotten to shut it all the way. I walked into the foyer and closed the door, locking it.

Yawning, I rubbed my hands along my face, massaging my cheeks. I decided the best thing for me to do was go upstairs and collapse on my bed. Allowing my body to feel the fatigue of my mind, I hoped maybe then I could relax, and lose myself in a good book.

When I opened my eyes, the alarm clock read one-twelve in the morning. After I shut off the light in the bathroom, everything was dark. I wondered why I turned on the light at night, when I should've just put a nightlight in the bathroom to see where I was going, and made a mental note to do that. I blinked several times to accustom my eyes to the darkness.

I put my arms out in front of me, trying to feel my way back to the bed, when something grabbed hold of my right arm, causing me to slip and fall to the floor.

My arms flailed as I searched in the dark, desperate to see what or who it was, and where they were.

Then he spoke.

"My dear Deanna, why do you have to meddle in other people's affairs? What will it take for you to leave and never come back?" the man said.

"Who are you?" I asked. "What do you want with me?"

"You couldn't just mind your own business, and go on with your life," he said, nudging my side with his boot. Not hard enough to hurt me, just enough to make me panic. "No!" he yelled, kicking at me a bit harder. "You had to interfere and cause problems. She was doing just fine until you showed up! Do you realize how long it took me to calm her down and forget about contacting you? Everything was in place, just as I planned, but then you had to move back here and ruin everything that I had worked so hard to accomplish. Now my question to you is, what do you think I should do about it?" he hissed. "But of course you will say that you will stop interfering, leave things the way they are, but it's too late for that now! You got the police involved, and they came and took her away."

"I'm sorry," I said, through my tears.

"Sorry doesn't cut it, Deanna!" he growled. "What you've taken can never be replaced. I know I should have disposed of you a long time ago, but you can thank your mother for that. That's if you ever see her again." I heard his footsteps as he moved around me.

"What do you mean, if I ever see her again? What are you going to do to me?"

"What I should have done years ago."

My eyes came into focus, and I could see his silhouette standing in front of me. He was tall and wide shouldered, but I couldn't make out his face, so I focused on his voice because I had heard it before. His hand reached down and grabbed a lock of my hair, forcing me to my feet then slammed me against the wall. I could hear glass breaking as the picture frame hit the floor. He placed his hand on my throat and slammed my head hard into the wall several times, and then tossed me to the floor.

I could taste blood in my mouth from when I bit down on my tongue. He knelt on top of me, and I felt something sharp on my face. My cheek was burning from a cut he made, and I could feel the warm blood pumping out. He took the knife, slicing my shirt down the middle, baring my breasts and stomach. His free hand glided down to my chest and around my breasts. He used the blade of the knife to trace in blood from my neck to my navel. I could feel the knife cutting my skin, and I thought of my son and wondered if I would see him again. I felt thankful that I had sent him to Brice's for the week, and was glad that I had opened up to Brice, and let him in. I was sad that I might not ever see him again. My mind blocked my thoughts, as I listened to what this man was saying to me.

"You look just as beautiful as you did all those years ago when I had you the first time, though you're more of a woman now. Your breasts are plumper and firmer than they were back then. I can still taste your scent on my lips. Oh, you taste so sweet and warm. It's a shame I have to kill you."

I tried to scream, but he clamped his hand over my mouth. He was licking the inside of my thighs, and then I felt him inside me. Hammering me. Pain shot up my navel as I continued to weep. My body was shaking; I couldn't keep from crying even though I didn't want to give this man the satisfaction of hearing my sobs as he continued to rape me. When he finished ejaculating on my stomach and chest, he pressed the blade deep into the skin of my chest. Every quick breath I inhaled ran through me like fingernails on a chalkboard. I could feel the blood pumping out from the cut he had made in my chest.

I must have passed out because when I opened the one eye that wasn't swollen shut, he was gone. Blood drizzled down the side of my face, as I lay helpless on my bedroom floor. I could still smell his scent on me. The same aroma I smelled so many years ago. I stretched my arm out in front of me and reached for the phone sitting on the nightstand. My fingers interlaced with the cord hanging down.

251

I yanked, but nothing happened.

Sharp agonizing pain surrounded my chest as I took in another breath. I pulled on the cord, once more.

The phone, now humming, was lying next to my face. I could taste blood running in my mouth.

My blood....

I flinched at the sound of a door slamming in the next room. *Is he gone? Did he leave me here to die?* I thought to myself.

I glided my fingers across the buttons.

"Nine-one-one, please state your emergency," the dispatcher said. Her voice was comforting to my ears. "Is there anyone there?"

"Help me!" I replied, though I sounded as if I were mumbling as my throat filled with blood and mucus.

"You called 911, is everything okay?" her voice, young yet high-pitched, echoed through the receiver.

Pain shot through me like lightning bolts; I cringed, and inhaled through my nose.

"Help me!"

"I heard you say you need help? Please stay on the line; I need to get some information," said the dispatcher.

"Are you hurt?"

"Yesss," I whispered, sounding like a snake as the air hissed out of me.

"Can you tell me what happened?"

"I…I have been stabbed. Please, you've got to help me before…" I was beginning to feel faint again and struggled to keep my eyes open.

"Is the person that hurt you still in the house?"

"I…I don't know." Wetness, like tears or maybe blood, beaded down my cheekbones and across my nose. "I think he left," I coughed and felt the blood splatter around me like an abstract piece of artwork.

"I have an ambulance on the way. I need for you to stay calm," the dispatcher continued to talk, but the pain became too overwhelming for me to respond.

Footsteps….

I heard footsteps coming towards me. His loud boots echoed through the floorboards, under my ear. I turned my head towards the ceiling. A shadow figure was standing next to me, hovering.

Pain jolted through the bones of my fingers, as he pressed his boot into my hand. I screamed. I could hear the dispatcher's frantic voice stream out through the telephone, and then she was gone.

I was alone fighting for my life.

The man threw the phone across the wall and it shattered to the floor.

"You are a bad, bad girl, Deanna," he hissed.

"Please!" I begged. "Please don't kill me, I...I promise not to tell anyone. I'll leave just like you asked." I thought for sure that I could talk him into it, at least long enough for the police to arrive and arrest him. I could see his leg rise up in the air, and then he slammed the heel of his boot into the side of my head.

I watched as the man stabbed me. My blood covering the floor, I asked, "Am I dead?"

The man looked up as if he heard me speak, and that's when I saw his face. I didn't want to believe what I was seeing. I had to be dreaming, but I knew this was real. I tried to move away from him, but I couldn't.

I just floated there, mid-air.

254

Part Three

The timing of death, like the ending of a story,
gives a changed meaning to what preceded it....

Mary Catherine Bateson

When you forgive, you in no way change the
past – but you sure do change the future....

Bernard Meltzer

29

I felt my chest jolt up like it was being electrified, then I heard someone say that she's back, let's get her to the hospital and prep her for surgery, and then everything went black, again....

I could hear something beeping beside me, and I opened my eyes. It wasn't pitch dark in the room; a beam of light streamed in from behind the corner of the curtain. Turning to my left I could just make out a figure sitting by the bed. *Do I know this person?* I thought.

I tried to think back in time, but nothing came to me. The person next to me spoke, but I wasn't sure who he was. He clicked on the light next to the bed, and I stared at him.

"Hey, Deanna. How are you feeling?" he said.

My mouth opened, but no words slipped out. I grabbed my throat with my left hand, and massaged it and tried again.

"Don't try and talk, I'll get you some water.

Your throat's dry, and you need to drink something." I focused on what he was doing, and wondered how I ended up here. After I drank down two glasses of water, I cleared my throat and opened my mouth to speak.

"Who are you?" I wasn't sure if he understood me as I heard the words whistle from my throat. He had a puzzled look on his face after I spoke, so I tried again.

"Who are you?" I asked.

"Deanna, it's me, Officer Bates."

How do I know that name? I wondered, as I scanned his face. *I don't know this man beside me.*

"You were badly hurt, and I've been waiting for you to wake up."

"Where am I?"

"You're in the hospital. You were attacked by an intruder in your house, but you were able to call 911 before it was too late."

"Too late for what? What happened to me? Why am I here?"

"Calm down, Deanna. Everything will be all right, and you'll be fine. We'll figure this out, and you'll remember in no time."

"Fine! Nothing is fine. I can't recall what happened to me!" This person named Officer Bates chuckled at what I said, and it irritated me.

"What's so funny?"

"You're the same Deanna I met a week ago, that's all."

"How long have I been here?"

"Going on two days. After they operated on you, you slept. I've been here every day to sit with you, hoping that you will wake up, and now you have."

"Why can't I remember you or what happened to me?"

"I'll have to get the doctor for that. I don't have those answers." He stood up and exited through the door on the other side of the room. I adjusted the bed to sit up, as sharp pain pulsated through my chest, making me catch my breath and hold it. Once it stopped, I sat back and waited for someone to return to the room. There were vases filled with flowers all around the windowsill, but only one caught my eye. It was a huge vase full of red and pink roses. I liked them best, and could smell their scent all the way over here in bed.

The door swung open and a doctor in a white coat walked in with the officer. She approached me, and I thought to myself how beautiful she looked.

"Hello, Deanna. I'm Dr. Sheldon; I've been taking care of you since you arrived. I'm glad that you have finally awakened."

"Do I know you from somewhere?" I asked. "You look familiar, but I just can't put my finger on it."

"Funny you should ask that. Your son and sister were here a week ago. You almost lived here, you were here so often."

My head was foggy now. "What has happened to me that I can't remember why I'm here?"

"It seems that you are suffering from retrograde amnesia."

"What is that?" I asked.

"Due to the trauma, your brain stopped collecting memories. That's why you don't remember what happened to you. When this occurs the last clear memory you have might be days, weeks, or even months ago, possibly years. Don't be surprised if you recall the good memories, and not the bad."

"Maybe if you tell me what happened, it will come back to me."

"We don't know all of it, that's something locked in your mind, and will come back in time."

"Okay, can you at least tell me what you know?" They looked at one another, and then back at me. Their puzzlement meant they didn't know if they should tell me everything or not.

The doctor cleared her throat. "There was an intruder in your house, but somehow you were able to call for help, and we have guessed that the police and ambulance scared him away. Though, when they got there, you were already dead. It took a couple of tries, but they were able to revive you in the ambulance. You sustained a head trauma, and I believe that was the cause of the amnesia," Dr. Sheldon said.

I turned toward the man's voice as he spoke. "We think you were thrown against the wall and banged your head. Broken glass covered the floor from the pictures falling from the wall. Do you recall letting this person into your house? The police checked every access, and there were no signs of forced entry."

I shook my head that I didn't, but I couldn't remember if I did or not.

"If you feel up to it, I would like to have one of the other doctors run a test on you. It may help you remember what happened that night," she said.

I nodded and laid my head back down on the pillow.

"Great, I'll send him in to see you." I stared up at the ceiling when she walked out of the room. I could hear her speaking with someone in the hall and telling him or her that they could come in and see me now, but that I might not know them. The man named Officer Bates stood when the door opened. He said that he would like to be present in case I said anything that could help with the case. I didn't turn to look at whoever it was that came into the room, because I didn't think I would even know the person.

When he spoke, I smiled. "Deanna, it's me, Brice. How are you feeling?"

A tear slid down my cheek as I lay there. It was my Brice. I turned and reached out my left hand to touch his face. How was it possible that I remembered him, but no one else?

"It's so good to see you, Brice." Someone else entered the room, but I didn't want to remove my eyes from him. He bent down and kissed me on the lips, and combed my hair behind my ear. I loved looking into those dark brown eyes; they were always so warm and sincere. A hand touched his arm and he moved to the side. More tears escaped my eyes when I saw my son's face and I grabbed his shirt, pulling him into me.

We both hugged and cried for a long time, until Brice cleared his throat, and asked Brent if he would mind stepping out for a few minutes, saying that he needed to talk with me alone. I kissed him on the cheek and he walked out, shutting the door behind him.

"What is it that you want to talk to me about?" I watched as he glared at Officer Bates, and then back at me. "What is it?" I asked, again.

"Do you mind if I talk to Deanna in private?" he asked Officer Bates.

"No, I guess not, but will your conversation be relevant to this case?"

He said no, and waited until the door closed, before he began. "Deanna, do you remember anything before I left? Let me state it in a different way. Do you remember giving me a piece of hair for a DNA test?"

"No, why do you ask?"

"When I came here last week, many events transpired and when Brent and your sister were in the hospital, a few new developments surfaced."

I listened as he talked about their accident, and my visiting Hank, and then Hank's murder. He filled me in on everything that I did up to the time I was put in the hospital. When he mentioned Dr. Sheldon, and my belief that she was my dead daughter, I was confused.

"Deanna, I got the DNA results back. I analyzed a piece of your hair and that of Dr. Sheldon's. I also did some other searches, and I found some information that I believe you should know."

Though I was confused by what he was saying, I realized that he may be telling the truth. Brice had never lied to me before, why would he feel the need to lie to me now. There were things I remembered and plenty I didn't, so I nodded and told him to continue.

30

Before he could say another word, the door lurched open and a man I hadn't seen before came strolling in with Officer Bates and my doctor. There was too much in my head now, it would just make me more confused if I thought about what Brice was trying to tell me.

"Deanna, I'm Dr. Hale. I will be the one to examine you during the tests we are about to perform on you."

"What kind of doctor are you?" I asked.

"I'm a psychologist. I have studied hypnosis for many years. Don't be alarmed; I am more than qualified to hypnotize you. There is nothing to be afraid of, and if you have any questions, please feel free to ask."

At the moment I couldn't think of anything, but that didn't surprise me. "No," I said, my mind a jumbled haze of thoughts, not memories, "I have no questions right now."

"Good. Then, shall we get started?" I nodded,

even though I considered saying no, that I needed more time. "It may take many sessions before we find the answers." Again, I nodded.

"Let me go over the definitions of hypnosis, so that you understand what I will be asking of you, and what will be going on when you are in a hypnotic state. Hypnosis is a state of deep relaxation combined with focused attention directed toward a specific goal. When a person enters hypnosis, there is a change in their brain activity, similar to that time just before sleep when the alpha state is entered. When you are wide awake, the beta brain wave state is predominant, but as you become more relaxed, it changes to alpha. During the alpha state, the mind is very open to visualizations and creating a rich sensory experience. You are up to two hundred times more suggestible while in the light state of alpha; it is not necessary to go deep into hypnosis for change to be possible. Everybody has the ability to enter a hypnotic state, and in fact, you already do this naturally several times a day without even realizing it. Like when you've been so engrossed in an activity, such as daydreaming or watching TV, that an awareness of your surroundings fades away."

"So, you're saying I will remember what happened to me?"

"Yes, in time you will relive what happened, but it may take several sessions before we make any progress," he responded.

"Okay, I think I can handle that."

"If the images start to become painful or you become frightened, I will pull you out. That is why this may take several sessions before we have our answers. Are you ready to begin?"

I glanced over at Brice, and he smiled at me, so I nodded, saying, "Yes, I think I am."

"Good, let's get started, shall we?"

I lay there listening as he spoke in a soft voice.

"Deanna, I want you to close your eyes and imagine that you are in a 'happy place' where you feel comfortable and secure, such as relaxing in a meadow beside a gentle running stream. Just let your feet and your legs relax. Feel your hips and your waist relaxing. Feel your chest and your arms going limp. Your shoulders, neck and head are letting go of all tension. Feel your entire body relaxing all over. You can feel a heavy, loose feeling coming over you. And as I continue to talk, that feeling will get stronger and stronger, until it carries you into a deep, peaceful state of hypnosis. Every word that I utter is putting you faster and deeper into that state. Sinking down and shutting down. And the deeper you go, the deeper you are able to go. And the deeper you go, the deeper you want to go and the more enjoyable the experience becomes. Now you are resting in a deep, peaceful state of sleep, going deeper and faster, until I bring you back. You will only accept those suggestions that are for your benefit and you are willing to accept.

Look around, can you tell me what you see?"

"I'm standing in my rose garden behind my house. My red roses have bloomed and the smell is sweet, and I inhale the scent through my nose, closing my eyes. A breeze tousles my hair as I stand in my back yard with my eyes shut."

"Good. Can you open your eyes and look around, tell me what else you see?"

"I see a door, but it's not the same door that leads to the kitchen, it is darker with no windows, I don't think it's even my house."

"Walk up to the door, Deanna, and turn the

knob. Can you open the door?"

"Yes, but there's no light. It's dark inside the room."

"Can you reach your arm out and flip on the switch?"

"Yes."

"What do you see, Deanna?"

"I see pictures on the wall; they're of me, when I was younger. I'm coasting down the hall, and I scope out a room. It is a living room and it reminds me of my parents' home. Picture frames are hanging on all the walls."

"Is there anything in the room that frightens you or makes you want to get a closer look?"

"Yes, a frame on the mantel. There is something different about it."

"Walk up to the mantel and hold that photo in your hand, tell me what you see, Deanna."

"It's a picture of my mom and sister, but it's not the photo of them that confuses me, it's the date on the bottom right-hand side."

"Can you read the date on the photo?"

"Yes, the year was two thousand-twelve. The

picture was taken just a year ago, which baffles my mind. The camera could have been set wrong, but something else is demanding my attention. I can still hear her voice as if she were there."

"The voice you are hearing is there. Turn around and follow the sound."

"In the corner where I came in, there is a woman. She speaks to me again, so I move towards her."

"What is she saying to you, Deanna?"

"You shouldn't be here, you know. He will hurt you if he knows you were here in his house."

"Who will hurt you, Deanna?"

"She doesn't say, she just tells me to leave and never come back, but I don't want to leave. I want to stay with her. I have missed her for so long; I don't want to live without her."

"Who do you miss, Deanna? Who is the woman talking to you?"

"My mother. She was killed in a fire ten years ago, but now she is standing in front of me. Older in appearance, but still as beautiful as ever."

"Did she tell you what happened? How she is alive, and not dead?"

"Yes, she told me that she was never in that house, that it was all a set up. But something is worrying me, like I did something to her, something I have done to cause her to leave me, and not tell me."

"What do you feel, Deanna?"

"I'm not sure. A man or a baby may have caused this. Maybe what happened when I was fourteen? I hear footsteps coming up the walk outside the house, and my mother turns off the light and pulls me up the stairs into a room. She closes the door and locks it, but then tells me to hide in the closet, so he won't see me."

"What are you doing in the closet?"

"I am hunched down in the corner hiding behind some clothes."

"Does this man come into the room?"

"No, not yet. I'm listening, waiting for him to enter the room, when I hear my cell phone vibrating."

"What do you do?"

"I look at it, but don't answer it."

"Who was calling you?"

"The name said Officer Bates."

"Did he know that you were going to this house?"

"No. We were supposed to go together, but he didn't show up at my house, so I left without him."

"Why did you need to go to this particular house?"

"I wanted to see what my sister was hiding."

"What do you mean, hiding? What made you think she was hiding something?"

"I had gone to her house once before to pick up her mail and noticed that everything was just the way my mother placed it in our home before it was burned. The same furniture and pictures on the wall. I came back to see the room upstairs that was locked on my first visit, the room I'm in now."

"Okay, now you are back hiding in the closet. What did you do after your phone rang?"

"I didn't answer it, but then it started to vibrate again."

"Was it Officer Bates calling you again?"

"No, it was a different number, a number that Officer Bates had given me. The call was coming from inside the house."

"Did you answer the call?"

"No, I turned off my phone and slipped it back into my purse. I didn't want the man in the house to know I was there."

"What are you doing now?"

"I'm pressing my ear up against the wall, trying to listen."

"Do you hear anything?"

"Yes, I hear the door unlock and squeak open, then footsteps."

"Are they coming towards you?"

"No, they stopped, he talks to my mother."

"Can you hear what he is saying to her?"

"No."

"Concentrate, Deanna. What is he saying to her?"

"I take in a deep breath and press my ear harder against the wall. Nothing, I can't understand what he is saying to her. I hear someone moving towards the closet and I collapse my body further inside. The closet door opens, I'm afraid."

"Take in a deep breath, Deanna. Tell me what you see. Do you see his face?"

"No, just an arm. He is telling my mother that he would like for her to wear the outfit he has taken from the closet then he shuts the door."

"What do you hear now?"

"Nothing, it is quiet in the room. Maybe he has left, but I'm not sure. I sit for a long time before my mother opens the door for me, telling me that it's safe to come out, that he has left. A light is on in the room and I can see newspaper clippings hanging on the wall, and my heart seems to skip a beat."

"What are in the clippings?"

"They are of me, every single one. There are so many photos of me, where I used to live with Brent."

"Is there anything else in the room that you see?"

"I turn towards a cloth curtain hanging from the ceiling in the corner behind me, but can't see what's behind it."

"Walk over to it, and pull the curtain away. What is behind the curtain?"

"My sister."

"Deanna, when I get to the count of five, you will be fully awake and feeling wonderful.

"One…two…three…four…five….

"Open your eyes, Deanna."

31

I allowed my eyes to focus, before looking around the room. I searched each face for a clue as to what had happened, what I may have said, but all I found was each face gawking at me. Then, I realized that I had told them I saw my sister and mother.

"How do you feel, Deanna?" Dr. Hale asked.

"Good, I feel good."

"That's great. I think we made wonderful progress today. Is there anything you would like to ask me?"

"Yes, I was wondering how it was possible to see something that I didn't recall seeing before."

"You mean looking behind the curtain?"

"Yes."

"Perhaps you wanted your sister to be there."

"What do you mean, I wanted it?"

Officer Bates replied, "After we talked on the phone earlier that day, before you were attacked, my Captain and several other officers went to the house. We found your mother there in the room upstairs, but there was no curtain, or your sister, for that matter."

"Okay, I'm not sure I understand. That doesn't explain seeing my sister under hypnosis," I said.

"I believe it was something you wanted to see, but you didn't in fact see it," Dr. Hale responded.

"So, you're saying she wasn't there?"

"That's correct, Deanna. I'm sorry, but we are still looking for her," Officer Bates added.

"But my mother is alive and well? Is she here now? Can I see her?"

"She's in a safe place, where no one can hurt her."

I glanced over at Brice, and he gave me a half smile. I recognized that he didn't know what to say to me. What could he say; there was nothing I could do but wait for the rest of my memories to return.

Dr. Hale left the room with Dr. Sheldon and Officer Bates. Brice moved in closer to me, kissing me.

"Deanna, are you okay?"

"What? Yes, I'm fine, Brice, just a lot to take in right now, that's all."

"I could imagine. It must be overwhelming for you, especially after waking up and being clobbered by all this information so soon. I love you and I am here for you, no matter what."

He slipped his hand in mine, and I squeezed it tight. "Please stay with me for awhile. I don't want to be alone."

He nodded and pulled the chair over to sit down. The door opened and my son glided in, making his way to the bed. I could see he was sad and didn't know what to say to me. What could a boy feel safe saying to his mother who has just awakened, and doesn't recall the events that have happened in the past week? I couldn't even remember him being in the hospital. I reached out to him, and he leaned in, hugging me tight. I whispered in his ear that I loved him, and he replied back, "I love you too."

Opening my eyes, I noticed Brice sitting next to me reading a magazine. I must have fallen asleep because when I looked toward the window I could see darkness descending.

"Where's Brent?" I asked.

"He went down to the cafeteria for something to eat."

"What time is it?"

"It's just after seven," he replied. "Are you hungry? Can I get you anything?"

"Water," I said. "I would like some water." He poured me a glass as I pushed myself up to a sitting position, and he handed me the drink.

"How are you feeling, Deanna?" he asked.

"I feel okay, I guess. Just tired," which was weird, considering I had slept for two days.

"You will be for awhile, I'm sure."

"Brice, why don't you take Brent and go home and get some sleep? You look exhausted."

He sighed then kissed me on the lips. "Look at you, always thinking about the people around you instead of yourself. I don't want to leave you."

"I know you're worried about me, but I'm safe now. No one is going to hurt me."

"I just think that you should forget about all of this and come back home. You and Brent can live with me. I have plenty of room at my house."

House. Something about that word bothered me, but I didn't know what. "Tell me again what I was doing this past week. Where did I go?"

278

"Why? Do you remember something?"

"I'm not sure, but when you said 'house,' something just didn't sit right." He started from the beginning, repeating everything that I didn't remember telling him before the accident. When he mentioned Hank and my going to his place, a glimmer of recognition surfaced, but what was it?

"What is it, Deanna?"

"I'm not sure, but…."

"But what?"

"Hank. What happened to him?"

"He was killed. Someone murdered him in his home out at the cemetery."

"Can you take me there?"

"Deanna, I can't take you out of the hospital. You're not well. You just woke up, and you have stitches all over your body."

"I'm very aware of that, but there's just an unsettling aspect to Hank's murder, and I need to go there." I knew he would fight me on this, but I wasn't in the mood to argue about whether I should go or stay. "I just need to see his place again. I need to see if I can identify anything there."

"Deanna, I think we should talk to the doctor about this first."

"No!" I said a little too loud. "She can't know, not even Officer Bates can know about this." The stare he gave me didn't concern me much because I already had my mind made up that I was going with or without him. I would prefer that he go with me, as I wouldn't be able to drive myself.

Minutes passed as he left the window and stood alongside me. "Okay, I'll take you, but then we are coming right back to the hospital."

"Agreed," I said. "Thank you, Brice."

"Sure, no problem, but just so you know, I'm only doing this because I love you and I want this to be over, and for us to have our life back."

"I love you too." He took a bag from the closet behind the door, and set it on the bed. The IV I'd had in my arm was taken out a few hours ago, so I didn't worry about walking with it. He helped me sit up, and I said I needed to use the facilities first, before getting dressed. My legs were a little wobbly, so he helped me to the bathroom, and back to the bed. I changed from my gown to the clothes that he had brought from home in the bag. He took off his jacket and slipped it on me, flipping up the hood to cover my head and part of my face.

We both jumped when the door sprung open to my room; it was Brent.

"Where are you going, Mom?" he asked.

Brice answered before I could get a chance. "Your mom thinks she remembers something and asked if I would take her to a place that could help her."

"And what were you going to do, just leave me here?"

"Sorry, we should have told you," I said.

"Sure, no problem. Well, if you're ready, let's go."

"You're not coming with us," I stated.

"Oh, yes I am. After what happened to you, I'm not letting you out of my sight."

"Fine. I'm not going to debate this with you, so let's go before someone realizes I'm gone." Brent left the room first to make sure the coast was clear, than waved us out. I hooked my arm through Brice's, while Brent led the way. Nurses walked by us, but no one gave us a second glance. Brice opened the car door and helped me into the front seat.

"Which way do I turn?" he asked as we exited the parking lot.

"Make a left; it's only ten minutes away." I wasn't sure how I knew where to go, it just came to me. I stared out the window as we drove down the road hoping that I would recognize something, anything. Nothing but houses flashed by me. Brice reached over and held my hand until I told him where to turn next. As we headed up Destiny Lane, I searched the darkness for answers, but didn't know what I hoped to find. As we neared a shack, I saw a flicker of light coming from the window, and then it was gone. I thought for a second that I was imagining it, but was certain that I hadn't. Someone was inside, but the real question was, who?

32

I looked over at Brice, and found him staring back at me.

"Shall we go in?" he asked.

I'd told him what I'd seen as we came up the drive, and said I wasn't sure whether we should proceed or not.

"We came this far, Deanna; I think we should at least check it out. It could give us the answers you've been seeking." He was right, but I wanted to recall the past week, and know why I felt a need to come here at all. I nodded, and we both pushed open our car doors. I gripped the frame, holding myself up, until Brice came over to help me.

"Brent, I want you to stay in the car."

"Hell no! This is exciting, like what you'd watch on TV, and now I'm living it."

I sighed; the kid had a point, but I was still his mother, so I answered, "True, Brent, but not funny."

We crowded together as we hiked toward the cabin. I whispered to Brice to peek into the window

283

first before we entered. Brent took my arm, and I leaned against the side of the building. I could feel the pain mounting, and fatigue was setting in.

"Mom, this place is creepy, but sort of cool at the same time."

I let out a small chuckle. Only my son would think that this was cool. Behind us, in a nearby tree I heard crows mocking us. The branches made rustling sounds as the wind picked up. What you might expect in a cemetery or out in the woods, but frightening. Brice came back over to us, shaking his head that he didn't see anything.

"Now what?" he asked.

"We go in and check the place out, I guess." We crept up the walk. Brice reached out to turn the knob, but the door squeaked open before he had a chance. It was pitch black inside, no glimmer of light at all.

"Please come in," the voice said. "I've been waiting for you to arrive."

I felt Brent come up beside me and squeeze my arm. He whispered, "Mom, are you sure we should do this?"

I wasn't sure, but there was something about the voice that sounded familiar to me, like I had heard it before. Then he spoke again, and I knew who it was.

"Deanna my girl, please won't you all come inside?"

"Hank, is that you? But I was told that you were dead!" Brice stood with his mouth open, waiting for me to say or do something. So, I took the first step inside.

Hank lit a candle and pointed us to the sofa near the window. "Please sit."

I limped over, rubbing my leg to get the shooting pains to stop, and lowered myself down on the couch next to Brent. My eyes roamed the room as I waited for Hank to take a seat across from us. I heard his knees pop as he squatted to sit. He was breathing heavy as if he were in distress.

"So, you knew I would come here, even after I was told that you were dead?" I asked.

"Yes, I knew you would figure it out, and come looking for answers."

"But I don't remember anything that we talked about or even coming here in the first place, for that matter. I don't know what has happened in the past week."

"You will, Deanna. It will all come back to you soon."

"How are you alive?" A flash of a memory came into my mind. I was sitting on a bench, and Officer Bates was next to me. I heard him tell me that Hank was stabbed several times, that he was murdered. In my hand I held a note, with my name on it.

"Deanna, is everything okay?"

I glanced around at all of them. "A remembrance came to me. It was when Officer Bates first told me that you were killed. He handed me a note that you had written."

"Oh, yes, the note that said to call you about the grave at nine on Monday."

"Yes, that's it, but you still haven't explained, how are you still alive?" I asked, again.

"You came here that day looking for answers about your daughter. You wanted me to dig up her grave to see if she was in the casket."

"Mom, what is he talking about? You never told me that I had a sister." My heart was racing. My past was coming back to haunt me because I'd chosen to keep this from him. I could see the shock and sadness in his face.

"Brent, I'm sorry. I should have told you, but she died when I was fifteen. I didn't think that her death would ever come up, at least not until we moved back here. I promise that I will tell you the whole story after we leave, but right now, can we please find out what happened, so I can remember again?"

"Sure, no problem." I wasn't convinced that he was fine with waiting, but what choice did he have.

"Okay, Hank, please continue."

"Where was I? Oh, yes, you came here because you wanted me to dig up her grave. Though I was hesitant about agreeing to do it, I know it meant a lot to you. After you left I made a phone call to a woman."

"Do you mean my supposed dead mother?" His rising brows creased his forehead when he heard my words.

"How did you know?"

"I went to Shelia's house, well, the house I thought was hers, but I found my mother there. She told me that she had talked to you that night," I replied.

"But you didn't say any of that when you were in hypnosis," Brice said. "Did you just remember that too?"

"I guess I did."

Hank covered his mouth and let out a deep cough. "Sorry," he said, and started where he left off. "Yes, I called your mother and told her that you were here and what you wanted me to do. She was the one who suggested that I call Officer Bates and fill him in on what we had discussed. I only did it for you, Deanna. I wanted you to stop searching for your daughter. I didn't want you to get hurt. You had been through so much in the past, and I wanted it to end. I was hoping that you would cease your search for answers, and move on with your life. Just like I tried to tell you to do before you left."

"So, you faked your death, and Officer Bates helped you?"

"Yes, it was all I could do to get you to stop this. What you find out won't make it all go away."

"Are you the one that put the letter in my mailbox saying, 'Get out of town before what happened to Hank will happen to you?'"

"Yes, I had Officer Bates place the letter in your mailbox."

I thought about what he was saying, but deep inside I still had this burning fire that was growing out of control. "Hank, I need you to tell me who was keeping my mother in that house."

"I can't do that!"

"Why not? Why is this man being concealed from me?"

"When the time is right you will find out, but right now you need to remember on your own what happened that night. And besides, she is in good hands, now that she is in a safe place. He can't hurt her anymore. Whether I should tell you this or not, it was never her."

"What's that supposed to mean?"

"It was always you that he was after."

33

"Me! Why me? What did I ever do to this person?" He seemed to listen to a sound coming from the far corner of the room. He quickly glanced at me as if hoping I didn't hear it too. "What was that Hank?" I asked.

"Nothing, probably just a mouse." Then I heard it again, it sounded like a moan. I stood, taking hesitant steps toward the sound.

"Dad, is that you?" the voice wailed. I stepped closer, until I was right next to the cot. I wasn't sure if it was the lack of light in the room or maybe even my mind playing tricks on me, again. I grabbed hold of the cot and knelt down. She and I were face-to-face now.

"Shelia, is that you?" I whispered.

"Deanna, what are you doing here?"

"I...I came to talk to Hank," I said, my mind growing hazy, the fog I was feeling refusing to lift, even as I stared at her.

Next thing I knew, I was sitting in a hospital room staring at my sister in a bed. There were monitors beeping, and I could hear people in the hall talking. There was a nurse standing on the other side telling me that she's in a coma, and that there was swelling around her brain. That once it goes down, she should wake up. I feel wetness on my cheeks as if I had been crying.

"Hey, Sis, are you there? What's wrong with you?" Shelia asked.

My eyes began to focus on her again. "What?"

"I asked if you were okay."

"Yeah, I'm fine, was having another one of those flashbacks."

"My dad's been taking care of me, ever since he brought me back to his place."

"Dad?"

"I was shocked at first too, but Hank explained everything. He told me about your mother and father adopting me when I was two. Now I know why we never looked alike or even acted alike while we were growing up. You would think I would be upset or angry, but I can see the reasons why I was confused when I was young."

"But you knew that mom was alive, and you didn't tell me?"

291

"You know?"

"Yeah, I found out by going to the wrong house to get your mail, and to make sure the house was safe."

"She made me promise not to tell you. I wanted to, but I saw my chance to be with her without you around. I hated how close you two were, and well, I just wanted her all to myself for a change." I remembered when growing up, how Shelia had treated me, how possessive she was towards my mother. A part of me wondered if I could ever forgive her.

"Hank already told me everything. My real mother died while giving birth to me, and he couldn't raise me living here. Not on his salary. He wanted me to have a good life, not one growing up in a cemetery. He knew your mother, and how she was having difficulty conceiving a child. He asked if she would consider adopting me, but then two years later she got pregnant with you. I'm sorry that I blamed you my whole life, Deanna. And I wish they'd told me about this sooner. This entire time I could've had the chance to know my real father and maybe I wouldn't have treated you like I did. A lot of that had to do with your father. But I guess like the old saying goes, things happen for a reason."

292

"I guess they do."

"So, how are you feeling? My dad told me that you were attacked in your home."

"I'm doing well."

"You never stop working, do you?"

"What's that supposed to mean?"

"It means even you need to take a break now and then. Quit being such a busybody, and enjoy your life."

"I do have a life now. Brice, can you come here please?"

"Brice is here?"

"And, Brent, too." I lifted myself up and sat at the foot of the bed while Brice and Brent visited with Shelia. I clenched my teeth as a surge of pain rippled through my chest, hoping I didn't rip out my stitches.

"So, you and Brice are a couple now?"

I giggled at the question. "Yes, we are a couple now."

"How are you feeling, Brent, since the car accident?"

"I'm fine. Can I still call you my Aunt Shelia, even though you're not?"

"I wouldn't have it any other way, Brent, my man." It was good to see her awake and talking, again. Brent and Shelia had a great time together. Always joking with one another, filling his void of being the only child. *Child, that's it!*

"Brice, you said you had the results of the DNA test?"

"Yes, I did."

"So, what were they?"

"Do you think now is a good time?"

"I don't know, but I thought I'd ask." He bent over and whispered that he'd rather not do it in front of Brent, that we should wait until later when we're alone. I nodded and looked over at Hank still sitting in his chair. He was quiet, a man of few words. There was something else that he wasn't telling me, and I thought about asking him. But it might be a waste of my time, considering he wouldn't tell me who was doing this to me. It seemed as if he would rather have me remember it, than to just come right out and tell me the truth. Something came to me, and I hobbled over to where Hank was sitting and sat across from him.

"Hank, I'm not going to act like I understand why you don't want to tell me who is doing this, but can you answer one question?"

I focused on his eyes as they moved back and forth, searching mine. "What is it, Deanna, my girl?"

"Will you tell me why my mother is alive, but my father isn't?"

"I think it's time for you to leave now, Deanna. I'm sorry, but I can't answer anymore of your questions."

"Who's Ann?" I blurted out, but wasn't sure where it came from.

"Ann? How do you know of Ann?"

"I don't know; it just came to me."

"Ann is the one from the newspaper," Brice said. "Who wrote about the doctor who adopted a baby." Brice and I must have been thinking the same thing because we both looked over at him at the same time. Brice walked over and took a seat next to me.

"What are you talking about?" I asked.

"It's one of the things you don't recall, but you did a search and found that she was the woman who wrote the article about your parents' death, and also about a doctor and his new baby."

I searched back in time trying to remember what he was talking about, but nothing came. "Hank, do you know Ann?" I asked, while observing his face.

"No, I don't know an Ann." Part of me wanted to believe him, but I had more doubt than anything. I knew in my heart he wouldn't tell me even if he did know. He wouldn't even tell me the name of the man who was after me.

"Deanna, I wish I could tell you everything, but it's for the best. You come back here after your memory returns. There's nothing more I have to say to you. I'm sorry."

"All right, we'll leave, but I will be back to finish this." Brice and I stood at the same time, and he helped me to the bed to say good-bye to Shelia.

Back in my room, Brice tucked me in bed. I was exhausted from the trip and needed to sleep. Kissing me, he said goodnight, and assured me that he and Brent would return first thing in the morning. I didn't want him to leave, but acknowledged that he needed his rest as much as I did.

Once he was out the door my eyes shut, and I was out.

In my dream I was standing outside my house, the first time I had come back here to move in. I unlocked the front door and went inside. Boxes were stacked against the wall in the living room, and through the hallway to the kitchen. I heard a noise and walked into the kitchen, gazing around. I could see myself putting glasses and plates away in the cabinets, humming to myself. Outside it was starting to get dark, but was still light enough to see. I moved toward the slider by the table and peered out. There was a person standing beside an old oak tree in the back yard. I could tell it was a man by his build. He was looking into my eyes.

As if my body were no longer mine, I felt as though I was hovering over the scene watching myself, looking at this version of myself standing by the sink staring out the window. *Could it be possible that I had seen him then too?* I wondered. He was still there when I looked back, but he was turning to leave. I opened the slider and called out, "Hey, who are you? What do you want?" But he was moving faster now, away from the tree. When I stepped outside a breeze pressed my dress against me, but when I looked down I noticed that I was wearing a hospital gown. I had no shoes on my feet, but I didn't care, I just wanted to find out who he was, and what he wanted with me. I leaped over the last two steps that led to the back yard, and ran to the tree where he was standing. I could see him about forty feet away from me, moving faster now. I yelled to him, but he didn't stop. I'm not sure why, but I called out a name, and that made him stop.

"Who are you?" I shouted.

"Go back to where you came from, Deanna," he answered, trying not to face me. "You have no business being here. Go back to the place you came from, and never come back." Then he was gone, and I was lying back in my bed with my arms hugging my chest, calling out to him.

"Dad, wait, come back!"

34

A nurse stood at my side, "Deanna, wake up. You're having a bad dream."

Sweat was rolling down my face and my gown was clinging to my skin. The nurse patted my forehead with a wet towel as I remembered what I just visualized. I had to go see Shelia again, and ask her if my father was still alive too, but I knew that they wouldn't let me out of the hospital.

"What time is it?" I asked her.

"It's three in the morning," she replied.

Way too early to call Brice to come to the hospital, so what else could I do but wait. After the nurse checked the bandages on my chest, she left. I turned on the TV, but found nothing on at this hour as I clicked through the stations, so I turned it off. Reaching into the desk drawer beside the bed, I pulled out a paper and pen and jotted down my dream, just in case I forgot. Setting the tablet next to me, I pulled the blanket up around me and closed my eyes. I heard the door to my room open, but was too tired to open my eyes, and thought it was probably the nurse coming in to check on me.

I felt a tiny prick in my neck, and my eyes sprang open to see what the nurse was doing, but it wasn't a nurse or a doctor. It was…

Fear flowed through me as I flashed back to the night I was attacked. The smell of his cologne filled the room. I felt my way through the darkness. He grabbed my arm, and I fell to the floor, then he threw me against the wall. I could hear him breathing in my ear, and his breath on my neck. Pictures fell from the wall and shattered glass covered the floor.

"You have been a bad girl, Deanna. Now, what should I do to you to teach you a lesson? A lesson you seem to have problems learning. I told you to leave that night, but no, you always have to meddle in other people's affairs. You didn't learn when you were fourteen. I had to teach you who the boss was. To have you learn that you do not sneak out of the house and go with boys. If it weren't for what I did to you, you would've continued to break the rules that I set and deceive me. That's right, all this time you thought that boy raped you, but he never knew what hit him when I came from behind that tree and smacked him in the head with a board, knocking him unconscious. And there you were lying there on that blanket with your eyes shut. Your skirt was pushed up high revealing your pretty panties; I couldn't help myself from being aroused by it. I've been watching you for years, as you've turned into a woman. Your own father raping you and you didn't even know it. And then, you became pregnant with our baby. I couldn't let you keep it and raise her. Do you know what people would have said if they knew you had your father's baby? I was the president of the school and a councilman of the town. We had to move because of you. Then, it hit me after you gave birth to her. I had to come up with a way to get rid of her. Do you understand? What would happen if she got sick, and they found out that I was the father? I would be ruined!

"The thing about being a well-known person is that you have people you can go to, to fix the problem. That's when Ann came into the picture. She was a nurse at the hospital where you gave birth, and she knew how to make your daughter disappear so no one would ask questions. She left after the baby was gone and waited for me until I needed her again. That's when she helped me and your mother disappear. Some people would call her a deranged loony, but you see, we loved each other, and she would do anything I asked her to do. Do you know who Ann is, my dear?"

I shook my head.

"She was my twin sister. She's the aunt you never knew, nor did your mother, for that matter. Well, until ten years ago when your mother took Shelia to the hospital for some tests and saw Dr. Sheldon. She came back to ask questions and found Ann and I together. She wanted to leave, but I wouldn't let her. I knew she would run her mouth and go telling everyone, especially you. So, I made her dead to the world. I kept her in a hotel room until I had the house finished. I sent a truck over to gather our things in the house, and moved them out here away from you. Then, I had Ann set the house on fire. That was most convenient, if you ask me. After the baby was adopted by Dr. Parka, Ann quit her job and started writing articles for the local newspaper."

My cheek burned from his slap. I was back in the hospital room staring straight at my father. "Dad, why are you doing this to me?"

"Do you really think I can let you live and tell everyone what I did to you? I can't allow you to do that. You had the police come and take your mother away from me, and now I don't know where she is. See, you've learned to live without her, but I can't, I need her with me. If she knew what I did to you back then and about the baby, she would have left me."

"Is that why she was always crying in the bathroom? You made her do things that she didn't want to do. All this time you kept her hidden in that house, away from me. You knew she would tell me the truth."

"Yes."

Hank had to have known this, and that's why he didn't want to dig up her grave. "Is my daughter still alive?"

"Yes, she's very much alive. And I must say that she is doing very well for herself, since Dr. Parka adopted her. It was his idea to give her a different last name, though I'm not sure why. Besides, she wouldn't have become anything if you had raised her."

"You don't know that."

"Don't I? All those times that you tried to commit suicide, Deanna? I think they would have found you an unfit mother after seeing those tapes."

My eyes were locked on his as he stood there smiling at me.

"Did I say something wrong?"

"How did you know that I tried to kill myself? What tapes?"

"The tapes from the camera I hid in your room. At first it was to watch you get undressed, but I recorded everything. God, you were so beautiful when you were naked. If it wasn't for your mother and Shelia finding out, I would have had you more often."

I wanted to lash out at him, but my body was becoming numb, and I couldn't feel my arms or my legs. I knew he was going to kill me; whatever he had in that needle was working, but not soon enough for him not to tell me everything. "You've been wanting to kill me all along?"

"I had to stop you from snooping around and discovering the truth, but you just wouldn't stop."

"And what do you mean she was your twin sister? What did you do to her?"

"Oh, Deanna, that's something you won't be alive to find out," his voice softened like he was seducing a lover. "You're starting to understand, aren't you, that I just can't let you live. When was the last time you visited your daughter's grave? I paid for it, so I might as well use it for something. It came in handy after you buried your not-so-dead daughter. I had to make the hole bigger, but that wasn't a problem. That's why the casket was closed when you went to her funeral. I took your baby out after the funeral and gave her to Dr. Parka." The tone of his voice began to shift. "The only flaw in my plan was Hank, that jackass who just can't stay the hell out of my family's life. And you had to choose a gravesite so close to that shack he calls home. I did him a favor by taking his daughter off his hands; all he had to do was keep his mouth shut. That poor soul was killed, you know. Someone broke in and murdered him. Serves him right."

He doesn't know that Hank's alive; that it was a set up just like he had planned ten years ago with the fire. "So, you were the one that took the book I gave my daughter?"

"I knew your mother would want it. She redid your old room just the way it was when we lived in the house you're in now. If that was what I had to do to keep her quiet, then so be it. Small price to pay to keep her with me."

"You did all this because I got pregnant? You used Levin and made him think that he was the one that raped me? Why were you there anyway?"

"I followed you everywhere you went with your friends. I had to know what you were doing. And as you got older, you were turning into such a beautiful girl that I just couldn't help myself. When you were at that party, and I saw you with that guy, I couldn't just let him have you first. Oh, no, you were mine!"

I couldn't believe my ears; my own father raped me. He raped me! Because of him, I'd been pregnant. I would have never had sex with Levin, not that young. "Did you drug me then too?"

"No, you did that yourself by drinking that beer he gave you. I must say, I didn't think you were such a lush. I watched him from the moment you two met at that party."

That night I thought my limited visibility was

306

from it being so dark out, but now I knew what I really saw. His face had become blurry, and it was hard to breathe as he lay on me. I tried to get him off, but he was too strong. I couldn't scream with his hand clapped over my mouth. Then it was over, and I lay there crying. When Levin approached me, his clothes were on and his forehead was bleeding. He tried to comfort me and I pulled away from his reach. I blamed him all these years, and he did nothing to me. My own father attacked me, and I never knew.

My body started to shake as if I was having a seizure. I tried to grab hold of his arm, but he stopped me. With all my strength I reached for my throat, felt it closing, and tried to breathe, but could only take shallow breaths. He pulled the needle from my neck and kissed me on my lips, then whispered in my ear, "Good-bye, Deanna, always know that I did this for you because I love you." My eyes watched as he left the room. I needed to stop him. My body started to go into convulsions.

The nurse, I have to get the nurse, I thought as I gasped for more air. I remembered seeing a call button somewhere on this bed.

307

A loud piercing alarm filled my ears. Did I hit the button?

Of that, I wasn't sure.

35

When I opened my eyes, I could see Brice staring down at me. I reached out to touch him, and he squeezed my hand in his.

"Don't worry, Deanna, everything will be all right. No one will hurt you anymore."

Was I dreaming this, or did I survive? I opened my mouth to speak to him, hoping that he was real, and that he could hear me. "My father's alive; he is trying to kill me," I said.

"Deanna, he can't hurt you anymore."

I didn't understand what he meant.

"You're alive, Deanna. We got to you in time," he said.

"I need to see my daughter; I need to tell her that I love her, and that I'm sorry for what he did."

"Let's wait until you are feeling better."

"You knew that she was my daughter. You tried to tell me."

"Yes, I did, and you can talk to her when you feel better."

"Who saved me?"

"Officer Bates was coming in to see you last night, when he noticed a man leaving your room, and then the alarm sounded. He rushed in as you were having a seizure. He waited until they were working on you, and then went after him. The man had dropped the syringe on his way out, and they were able to know how to save you. Officer Bates caught him before he was able to escape the hospital and took him to jail. He can't hurt you anymore."

"My father told me that he was the one that raped me, not Levin. He planned it. He said that he followed me everywhere I went, and that he couldn't stand to see me with anyone else. That he had to have me."

"Deanna, I knew."

Brice stepped aside, and I saw Officer Bates behind him in the corner. Brice nodded at him, and left the room.

"What do you mean, you knew?"

"Deanna, I wanted to explain that day we talked in the parking lot, but I just couldn't bring myself to tell you. I could see how upset you were getting when the name Levin came up, so I lied and told you my name was Michael."

"What are you saying?"

"That I am Levin. The same Levin you met that night at the bonfire and the many nights following. I knew you wouldn't believe me if I told you that I didn't rape you. That someone else was there that night. I thought if I let you remember on your own, that you would know it wasn't me, but you never allowed yourself to see it."

I couldn't believe what I was hearing, though it wasn't as much a shocker as finding out that my father was the one who took everything from me. I searched his face to identify him as Levin and noticed the one mark that made it all true. The scar on his forehead was there all along.

"Deanna, I'm glad that you came back to this town."

"Why are you glad?"

"Because I always wondered what happened to you and what you were doing with your life," he said.

I wasn't sure how to feel at that moment, with this man I once cared for opening up to me. Telling me that he'd never stopped thinking of me. And yet, throughout my life I had always blamed him for what

311

happened to me back then, until last night. "I don't know what to say to you after all these years."

"I don't blame you for thinking it was me. I just wanted you to be happy."

"I will be after I get out of this place." We both laughed, and he bent down, giving me a hug.

"Will I ever see you again?"

"That I couldn't tell you. After I'm discharged, I think I'm going back to where I came from. This isn't where I want to be, even though I once thought it was."

"That's understandable."

"There's one more thing I need you to do for me."

"Sure, what is it?"

"I know this will sound strange at first, but I need you to go to the cemetery, and dig up a grave."

"Why do I need to do that?"

"Remember I mentioned a person named Ann?"

"Yes."

"Well, my father said that he had to make the hole bigger, and something tells me that she is buried there." I filled him in on everything that he'd confessed to me, and who Ann was.

"I'll check it out for you."

"Thank you, Levin, I appreciate your protecting me."

"Of course, no problem."

I could see a slight frown surface on his face. There was something else he wanted to add, but didn't. After finding out what happened that night so long ago, I wasn't sure how I felt about Levin. I loved and cared for him so much, but now, now, there was nothing in my heart for him.

"Take care of yourself, and I wish you all the happiness in the world."

"Thank you, Levin." He stopped before he reached the door, and turned, saying, "I just want you to know that I never stopped thinking about you and that you will always have a place in my heart." He opened the door then stepped out, letting it shut behind him.

I lay there thinking about what Levin just said and everything that had happened. Finding out about my father, and what he did to me I would not forget, but I refused to live the rest of my life dwelling on what he did. I'd already spent over half my life blaming the wrong man. Then, it hit me, an uncertainty if I should even say anything to Dr. Sheldon about being my daughter. Or, if I should just let it go. I couldn't leave without her knowing that I had always loved her, and that her mother was here and alive.

Could I?

36

Brice helped me out of the car after returning home. I had him schedule a moving truck to come and pack our belongings as we would move back home with him. It's where Brent and I belonged, I told him. It's where I wanted to be.

Hank, Shelia and my mother were waiting inside when I opened the door. Shelia had decided to stay here and get to know her father and make up for all the years they hadn't been together. As for my mother, she would be moving back with us, into the house I still owned. I had Brice call and tell the realtor to take it off the market. My mother said she didn't want any of her possessions from the house, except for a few photos.

Brent had a different attitude since our last encounter and had changed tremendously. After finding out the truth that I had hidden from him all these years, he seemed to understand what I'd been living with. He has been so thoughtful and helpful to me, I couldn't ask for a better son.

As for Dr. Sheldon, I knew in my heart that I would always cherish her as my daughter, but for some reason I couldn't find it in me to change the world she now lives in. She has worked so hard to become the woman she is, and who am I to take that away from her. Maybe one day she will learn the truth.

In my hand, I held an envelope with her name on it. It contained a letter that I wrote my last day in the hospital. It explained everything that has happened in the past two weeks. I placed it in a box filled with items I had bought for her when I was pregnant and included the book then sealed the box, writing her name on the lid. I placed it in my office to be packed with the rest of my items.

After I woke up from a nap, Brice decided to take us all out for dinner that night to celebrate everyone's new beginnings. I sat smiling at each one of them, picturing the life we will now lead, and praying that we will continue to be happy and healthy. Brent was smiling and laughing again, something that I hadn't seen in so long. Brice reached over and kissed me on the lips and slipped from his chair to one knee.

For a moment, I wasn't sure what he was doing until he flipped open the lid of a small box. Nestled inside was a sparkling heart-shaped diamond ring with rubies and diamonds staggered on each side.

"Deanna, I love you more than words can say, and I can't imagine my life without you. Will you do me the honor of becoming my wife? Because I sure want to be your husband!"

I giggled through the tears running down my face. I couldn't remember a time when I was happier. "Yes," I replied. "I would love for you to be my husband." He slipped the ring on my finger and kissed me with passion on the lips. I could hear my son cheering across from me, saying that it was about time. People all around us were clapping. I couldn't imagine my life any sweeter then it was right now, but I was wrong. Sitting there with my family, I thought of her.

37

Tomorrow the movers were coming to pack, so we said good-bye to Hank and Shelia, but before she left I asked her a few questions about issues that weren't resolved.

"How did my father not know you visited Mom?"

"I hid it the same way you did. I went when he was out working, and I gave her a cell phone so we could talk every day.

"But how did you know she was alive?"

"Believe it or not, it was at our old church."

"What do you mean?"

"After my husband died, I would go there and sit inside for hours. One day when I was there, I heard the door shut from behind me. At first, I just sat there lost in my own thoughts, and the next moment, she was sitting beside me. We talked for quite a while. After the initial shock wore off, she made me promise not to tell you, but she wouldn't tell me why. What else could I do? I had always craved her attention, and it seemed like the right thing to do at the time. I should have told you that she was alive, but I made a promise."

"That explains why Pastor Patten looked confused when I told him that our parents died ten years ago."

"Yeah, he had seen us there every week; it was the one place your father allowed her to go without him. I'm sorry I didn't tell you. She said he would hurt you if you knew she was alive, but don't you let this bother you. You have a great guy who loves you, and your father is far away from here, and can't hurt you any longer."

"Okay. I just wanted to know what your part was in this."

"I think you can talk to mom about that now, and she will always be there for you. You were always her number one, and I accept that now; besides, I have my real father to get to love. You went to that house, not by mistake, but as fate. It was time for you to find out that she was alive and well and I'm grateful that you did. It was a hard secret to keep from you because I knew how much she meant to you."

"But why didn't you stop him from doing what he was doing? Why didn't you go to the police, and get her out of there?"

"I know you don't understand my actions, but Mom promised me that he wasn't hurting her, and that I shouldn't do anything except what I was already doing. Mom thought I would go ballistic about being adopted, but I'm not upset. After finding out, I was relieved to know that my father didn't have a choice at the time, and he wanted me to have a good life. I'm sorry I treated you the way I did growing up. It doesn't make up for what I said and did to you, but I do hope one day you will find it in your heart to forgive me. Believe it or not, Deanna, I almost died in that hospital, and Hank coming there, and taking me home, was what I needed to save me."

In all reality, she was right. Even though we didn't get along when we were young, that was one trait about her I liked. As she got older, I could see the change in her from when we were kids.

As for me, I was starting a new life, and for once I am happy; besides, what more could I need when I have Brent and Brice, the two wonderful men in my life that love me?

I hugged Shelia one last time, and we both made a promise to keep in touch with one another. I said good-bye to Hank and walked them both to the door.

Standing outside, I waved them off and turned to head back inside. A beam of light lit up the wall of the house, and I peered over my shoulder. I thought maybe they had forgotten something and came back to retrieve it. So, I stood and waited, but it wasn't Shelia or Hank that appeared in front of me.

"Deanna, I read the letter you wrote," Dr. Sheldon said.

If she was talking about the letter I put in the box in my office, I didn't believe her, but there was no other letter that she could be referencing.

"Why didn't you tell me?" she asked in a soft voice. "Were you just going to leave without saying a word?"

I wasn't sure where to go with this, but I had to tell her the truth, once and for all. "Please come in and sit, I have so much to tell you." Brice was playing a video game with Brent upstairs and my mother was lying down, so we wouldn't be interrupted.

She followed me into the kitchen, and I asked her if she would like some hot tea. She replied yes, and I turned on the top burner to heat the kettle. When I turned around, I saw her holding a box under her arm.

"What do you have there?" I asked.

"It's the box you had sent to the hospital."

"I didn't send any box." I flicked on the light in my office. On the desk where I had placed the box, was a vacant space. I thought I was going to lose my mind; I headed back to where I left her and asked to see the box. As soon as she handed it to me, I knew it was the same one. I wasn't sure how she got it, but was certain it had to be Brice or Brent, and would ask them later.

"Please have a seat while I finish preparing the tea."

A few moments later, I set a tray with creamer, sugar, and a hot pot of water on the table. I poured us each a cup and sat down across from her.

"I'm not sure where to start," I said, feeling a lump surface in my throat.

She handed the envelope to me. "I would like for you to read this out loud to me."

My hand was shaking as I gripped the envelope and retrieved the letter from inside. Clearing my throat, I began to read to her.

My Darling Daughter,

I named you Kimberly Rose, after my favorite flower. The first moment I saw you, I decided you were the most beautiful baby I had ever seen. I was fifteen years old when I had you. I wasn't even old enough to take care of myself, much less a baby, but I wanted to raise you. I was told when you were born, only minutes after I held you, that you had died from heart failure.

I loved you so much it destroyed me when you left this world. I eventually got through the pain of my loss, and made a life for myself. Not a day went by that I didn't think of you, and wonder what you would have been like as a child, a teenager, and an adult. Holding you in my arms for that short time, I knew I couldn't love anyone as much as I loved you.

Right now, I sit here and think back on how tiny your little fingers were and how you would wrap them around mine so tight, as if you were afraid to let go. Your eyes were the prettiest blue I'd ever seen and I can see that they haven't changed. Your hair was just as black then, as it is now. I read to you every day and night, though you were just a tiny seed inside me, growing each day. I knew deep inside that you didn't comprehend, but you could hear me. I thought of you always. And I am proud of the woman you have become.

I know you don't understand any of this right now, but what I'm about to tell you might hurt you, which is the one thing I never wanted to do. The day we met at the hospital, and I saw your face for the first time. I could feel that you were mine, but I had no evidence.

You looked exactly like me. But it wasn't until yesterday that I found out what had happened back then, and why.

Even though I am writing this letter to you, I'm still not sure whether I will give it to you. It's been twenty-six years, and you have grown up. You made yourself a life, one that I wasn't able to give you.

  You may ask yourself, why wouldn't I tell you that I am your mother? For many reasons. To start, I haven't been a part of your life since you were born. You were taken from me before we could even get a chance to know each other. If I could've changed that I would have, but it wasn't for me to alter. I guess that's why they say things happen for a reason.

  You have a life that I didn't give you, and I don't want to ruin what you have. But if I ever am able to tell you my thoughts in person, I will say that I love you more than you will ever know, and you are not forgotten.

Love, from your mother,

Deanna

I lay the letter down on the table and looked over at my daughter, who was seeing her mother for the first time. I wasn't sure what to say to her that I hadn't already said in the letter. I could sit here all night staring at her, and we wouldn't have to talk at all. It may sound quaint, but to be sitting here in front of my first-born child that I thought was in heaven, is such a blessing in disguise.

About the Author

Donna Zadunajsky was born and raised in Bristolville, Ohio. She is 41 years old and resides in Homer Glen, Illinois. Ever since she was a teenager, she had an interest and a dream to write books. Six years ago that dream came true. She has written seven children's books that are about her daughter and all the adventures that she has done in her young life. They are currently on the Barnes and Noble and Amazon website and at www.littletscorner.com., available in eBook and paperback.

She spends her time writing short stories as well as novels. She published her first novel, "Broken Promises," June 2012, and has currently finished her second novel "Not Forgotten".

Besides writing, she enjoys spending time with her twelve-year-old daughter and her husband, their two dogs and two cats. She enjoys reading and working on crafts and scrapbooking. She graduated from The Institute of Children's Literature, in spring 2011.